ROPED IN

An ARMED AND DANGEROUS novel

L.P. DOVER

Roped In
L.P. Dover
Copyright 2015 by L.P. Dover

Editor: Victoria Schmitz at Crimson Tide Editorial
Cover Design by: Regina Wamba www.maeidesign.com
Model: Joshua Gawrysiak
Interior designed and formatted by

E.M.
TIPPETTS
BOOK DESIGNS

www.emtippettsbookdesigns.com

This book is dedicated to my oldest daughter, Abbey. She told me if I ever wrote about a singer, I needed to dedicate the book to her since she loves to sing. I'm living up to my promise. Singing has always been a passion of hers and mine. I really hope she follows her dreams.

CHAPTER 1

HADLEY

"*Hadley! Hadley! Hadley!*" the crowd cheered.

I blew a kiss and waved. "Thank you for joining me tonight. I love the energy here in Los Angeles! I have to say, I've missed this place. Make sure to listen to the radio this week for the debut of my new song, *Whispered Words.*"

"Sing it now!" one of the fans shouted. It was a little girl with blonde braids and freckles, sitting on her dad's shoulders. She reminded me of myself many years ago, when I stood in almost the exact same spot, watching my idol, Martina Hill perform. One of these days, I was determined to do a duet with her.

I winked at the little girl and shook her tiny hand.

"I wish I could, sweetheart, but it has to be a surprise." Then I lifted my gaze to the thousands of fans in the stands and waved again. "I hope you all like it. Goodnight, everyone." They went wild and I laughed as I ran backstage.

Waiting for me at the edge of the stage with a huge smile on his face was the love of my life, Nick Meyers. No one could resist his tousled, chocolate brown hair and gorgeous green eyes. The ladies loved him, almost as much as they hated me for having him.

"You were on fire tonight," he shouted.

Rushing off stage, I jumped in his arms and squealed. "What are you doing here? I thought you weren't going to be able to make it."

Cameras flashed and he grinned, his eyes twinkling mischievously. "I can leave if you want," he joked, releasing me from his grasp.

I gripped his arm and pulled him back to me. "Definitely not. What would the press think?"

Chuckling, he bent down to kiss me, knowing the reporters were taking note of our every move. "Was that a good enough kiss, or do I need to make it more convincing?" he asked, whispering in my ear.

Rolling my eyes, I playfully pushed him away. "I think you need a cold shower."

"Care to join me?" he quipped, waggling his brows.

"Right now, we have work to do. Get your head out

of the gutter." We faced the reporters and he held me close as questions were thrown at us in rapid fire. A lady with bright red hair and huge glasses, pushed through the crowd and held out a recorder. "Miss Rivers, we've heard rumors you and Mr. Meyers are engaged. Is that true?"

Nick smirked down at me and I held back a snicker. It was crazy how rumors got started out of nowhere. The next thing I knew, we'd be married and having a baby. "If she was engaged," Nick began, "I would definitely be letting the world know."

We answered several more questions before it was time to go. I knew I was going to have a gazillion autographs to sign on the way to the dressing room. Relaxation was something I needed to schedule now, or it would never happen. I had to get home and get rested up before my early flight to Texas.

Nick was always patient with me when dealing with the press, but I did the same for him too; he was just as famous. I was a rising, country starlet with one of the best hockey players in the country as my boyfriend. Unfortunately, our romance was all for show, but we played the parts beautifully.

Once we were behind closed doors, I breathed a sigh of relief. "The questions keep getting more outrageous don't they?"

"Same shit show, different day." He helped me pack

up my things and stuffed them into my bag.

"I thought you were busy with the team tonight?"

"I was, but I made sure to get away early. I missed my buttercup."

I rolled my eyes, nudging him with my elbow when he pulled me into his arms. "You have a life too, Nick. I don't want you sacrificing everything to be with me. You should've stayed with the team."

"Trust me, baby, I'm not sacrificing a single thing. I enjoy every minute of it."

"Even if you don't get anything in return?" I asked, lifting my gaze to his.

For the last four months, he was mine, but not really. It was his and his sister's idea for him to be my fill in boyfriend. His sister, Felicity Myers, was also my agent and the one who'd introduced Nick to me. I guess they were right, it was safer for people to see me with someone, instead of single and living alone. And I enjoyed having him with me, but I didn't want to drag him into the danger surrounding my life.

His smile faded, his gaze serious. "I get plenty in return, Hadley. I'm happy where I'm at, even if I have to steal your kisses. It's not *that* bad being with me, is it?"

"Are you kidding? You're gorgeous and could have any woman you want, but yet you choose to be stuck with me. It makes no sense."

"It does to me," he murmured.

"I've asked you this before, but I need you to be honest with me." He sighed and nodded for me to continue. "What did Felicity promise you? Surely you didn't just agree to be with me for nothing in return." I had often thought about what it would be like to take things further, but I didn't want to ruin our friendship. When I met him two years ago, we instantly clicked. I considered him more of a best friend than a lover.

Grazing his finger across my cheek, he answered, "My sister didn't promise me anything. I offered to do this. Believe it or not, I like being with you. At least it's gotten that fucking psycho off your back." And there it was, the sole reason for the mess I was in.

"So we *think*," I corrected. "What happens when we can't keep this ruse up? What if he comes back?" What started out as innocent letters had quickly turned into stalking, then to trespassing. Presents were left on my doorstep, and the ever watchful eyes of that creeper could be felt every time I left the house. It got to the point where I was scared to be alone. I used to be able to run around my neighborhood and go shopping by myself, but I couldn't anymore.

Nick stepped closer. "That bastard isn't going to get near you as long as I'm around. I believe this plan will work. Eventually, this guy will give up and find someone else to fuck with. Now stop thinking about him, there's something I wanted to talk to you about and I'm not going to do it here."

"Oh yeah? What is it?"

"You'll just have to find out. Come on," he said, opening the door.

There were two security guys standing by the door, I nodded at them as we passed. Their steps could be heard on the concrete floor, following closely behind. I never thought having a security team was important, until I heard horror stories from other singers. Luckily, I hadn't had anyone break into my house to steal my underwear like my nemesis, Lydia Turner. The attention she got after that incident, inflated her already enormous head. I would've been scared shitless to know some pervert was in my house. Not her; it was just another way to get free PR.

"Where's Scott? He usually comes inside to get me," I mentioned.

Scott Wilson worked security for my father, until he'd been sent to protect me. I didn't mind having a bodyguard, but I had boundaries. Thankfully, Scott and I had come to a shaky agreement; he wouldn't hover, unless I wanted him to. He loved to test my patience though.

"He's waiting out by the car. When I came in through the back, I told him I'd bring you out."

"Wow. Hopefully, he's taking what I said to heart."

Nick shrugged. "Possibly. You ripped him pretty

hard the other night. The guy's just trying to do his job."

I sighed. "I know, and I hate how I took my anger out on him and not my dad. Scott's a good guy. I just wish the whole country didn't think I got my career because of my dad and his money."

"They don't. Did you not hear the thousands of fans cheering for you tonight? You have an amazing voice. Money can't buy what comes naturally. Besides, you know why your father's so protective."

I leaned into his shoulder, as memories of my mother came flooding back. It had only been two years since we'd lost her to cancer. The first song I ever wrote was about my parents' love for each other; it was what skyrocketed my career. It didn't help I looked exactly like her. My father couldn't look at me without the pain showing on his face.

"I know," I whispered, blinking back the tears.

Once we were out the back door, there were more security guards who flanked us as we walked toward the car. Up ahead, Scott straightened his suit jacket and opened the car door. He was in his early forties, with a closely shaved head and an athletic build. In New York, he didn't have to worry about the paparazzi taking his picture. Now, he was all over the tabloids as one of the sexiest bodyguards alive.

"You did well tonight, Hadley," he said.

"Thanks, Scott. I really appreciate that. But what I

want to know is, how are you going to chase down the bad guys in a suit?" I winked and it made him smile. The last thing I wanted was tension between us when he was obviously going to be working for me long term.

"You'd be surprised what all I can do. But hopefully, we won't have to find out. Get in."

I slid into the car and Nick scooted in next, putting his arm around me as soon as he settled into the seat. Once Scott got in the front, we headed out for the thirty minute drive back to my home in Santa Monica.

"I take it you're not mad at me anymore?" I asked Scott.

He chuckled. "It's hard to stay mad at you, kid. You just need to understand, I have a job to do."

"I know," I said with a nod. "I'm sorry for being a bitch."

His gaze met mine in the mirror. "You're forgiven." All too soon we arrived at the house and he parked the car. "You two have a good night. If you need me, you know where I'll be."

I nodded. "See you in the morning." Nick opened the car door and helped me out.

Scott got out of the car and headed to his apartment over my garage. "Be ready by seven, Hadley. We don't want to miss our flight."

I saluted him. "Yes, sir."

Grinning, he shook his head and disappeared into

the garage.

Nick slid his arm over my shoulders and squeezed. "Babe, you ready?"

"Yeah, let me get my keys." We started for the door while I dug in my purse, my heart thundering out of control. Was I ready to hear what he had to say? "So . . . what did you want to talk about?" I asked, voice shaking.

Chuckling, he stopped mid-step. "Nervous much? Surely you must already know." His expression turned serious, his fingers made their way to my cheek.

I *was* nervous, but not in the way he assumed. "Please don't do this, Nick. It'll only complicate things."

"How? When I'm not at my games, I'm with you. Everyone thinks we're together. Why can't we make this real?" Body tense, he stared at me with those blazing green eyes of his. "Is it really just an act with you?"

My heart ached but my decision was firm. I knew he had feelings for me, and I'd made damn sure I didn't fall for him. "It's not all an act, but you're my friend. Being with me will only tear us apart. The media has already tried, you know that. We don't need feelings clouding our judgment."

He scoffed. "Speak for yourself." I watched his jaw muscles clench; it was something he did when he was angry.

"Hey," I murmured, "I *do* need you. But the last

thing I want is to jeopardize what we already have." He lowered his gaze at my words. "Now let's go inside and eat some Ben & Jerry's. It'll help clear our minds."

"You got anything for an aching heart? You're killing me here."

I shook my head. "I'm sure you'll be just fine. Now, come on. There are countless girls who'd kill to be yours. It will be easy to forget about me."

Sliding the key in the door, he mumbled under his breath, "Not going to happen," but I pretended not to hear. My heart already hurt enough for him. Inside, the house was pitch black. That was strange. I always kept lights on. Sliding my hand against the wall, I found the switch and flipped it. Nothing.

"Is the power out? I don't remember seeing the rest of the neighborhood this dark."

Nick followed me into the house. "No, the other houses have their lights on," he said, pointing to the neighbor's house through the window. "Let me get a flashlight." Shuffling through the kitchen, he pulled out our junk drawer and grabbed the flashlight we kept in there. He turned it on and brought it over to me. "Maybe the breaker tripped. Wanna check it out with me?"

"Sure," I laughed. "I'm sure Scott will be busting through our door any second." We started for the laundry room, but then a sound above caught my attention. "What was that?" Frozen in place, I kept my gaze on Nick. My heart pounded so hard, I felt sick.

Nick glanced up at the ceiling, eyes blazing. The footsteps were light, but audible as an intruder moved around. "Get out of here, now," he hissed low. His fingers dug into my arm and he pushed me out the door.

I kept hold of his arms. "I'm not leaving you."

He jerked out of my grasp and clutched my face, his grip firm. "Stop being so fucking stubborn. Go get Scott and call the police, now!"

Turning his back on me, I got one last look at him before he disappeared into the darkness. I ran out of the house, hands shaking as I tried to dig for my phone. It felt like I was running through quicksand, similar to that feeling you get when running away from someone in your dreams. You can never move fast enough.

"Hadley!" Scott shouted, rushing out of the garage. I ran to him and he pulled me to the side, shielding me.

"Someone's in the house. Nick's still in there," I cried, my hands shaking out of control.

"Go next door and call the police. Don't step out until I come for you." Once I nodded, he took off inside the house.

Determined, I ran as fast as I could to my neighbor's house. By the time I reached their door, I'd found my phone and called for help.

"911. What's your emergency?"

"I'm Hadley Rivers and someone's in my house.

Please send help." I gave the operator my address and hung up just as my neighbor, Gabriella Emerson, opened the door. She was dressed in her workout clothes with her midnight colored hair pulled high into a ponytail.

Her smile disappeared the second she looked at me. "Oh my God, Hadley, what's going on?" she demanded. She quickly dragged me inside, and her husband, Paxton, hurried over. They were both MMA fighters and had seen their fair share of violence over the years. If anyone could help, it'd be them.

"Someone broke into my house. They're still in there," I shouted.

Gabriella grabbed my hands and squeezed. "Calm down, honey."

"I can't! Nick and Scott might be in trouble."

Paxton started for the door. "I'm going over there."

"Pax, wait!" Gabriella called. He took off and she huffed. "Dammit, why doesn't he ever listen?" She rushed out after him and so did I.

Scott had told me not to leave their house, but I couldn't listen. Again, it felt like everything moved in slow motion. I couldn't get to them fast enough. Before we could reach the edge of my yard, a gunshot fired from within my house and I screamed, ducking down to the ground. Paxton and Gabriella did the same and crouched low. Dread settled into the pit of my stomach as another shot fired, and another.

I had to make sure they were okay. Charging toward my house, I didn't get very far until Gabriella tackled me to the ground.

"Dammit Hadley, you're not going in there."

"Nick! Scott!" I shouted.

I tried to fight her off, but there was nothing I could do against an MMA fighter. Paxton glanced back at Gabriella, a silent plea on his face; Gabriella nodded. "Go."

"Nick doesn't have a gun. What if he's hurt?" I cried. Gabriella loosened her grip, but kept a vigilant watch of the house. I wished I was strong like her. I'd be able to take care of myself instead of having others do it.

"Don't worry, everything's going to be fine," she said, but even I could hear the uncertainty in her voice.

"Gabby!" Paxton yelled from inside the house. "I need help in here."

She jerked me to my feet and we both took off for the house. When I got inside, the smell of blood was overwhelming. Everything came crashing down the second I saw Scott and Nick on the floor, covered in blood. But it was Scott who was unmoving, lifeless, his unseeing eyes staring up at the ceiling.

"Scott!" I cried. Paxton rushed over and took his pulse. The pained look on his face was answer enough. I stumbled over and fell to my knees beside him. "He has to be alive." But he wasn't; he was gone.

"Hadley," Nick croaked. Gasping, I crawled over to him and placed a hand over his. Blood oozed out of the wound in his gut. He glanced over at Scott's still form and closed his eyes. "He . . . saved me."

"Where did the shooter go?" Paxton demanded.

Nick swallowed hard. "Back door." His eyes rolled into the back of his head and his body shook.

"Nick! Hang on, *please*," I cried. Putting my hands over his wound, I attempted to stem the blood flow.

Sirens blared down the street, but they were going to be too late.

Growling, Paxton dashed toward the back door. "I'm going after the fucker."

Tears streamed down my cheeks as I watched Nick's life slowly slip away. Gabriella rummaged through my house and came back with a towel. I took it from her and placed it over the wound.

"Nick, stay with us," Gabriella commanded, as I applied pressure to the wound. It seemed to help, but what did I know.

He turned to me, his sea green eyes glassy and full of tears. His body stopped convulsing, and was replaced with a sense of calm. "I wanted . . . to protect you."

"Did you see who it was?" Gabriella asked softly.

He closed his eyes, his grip on my arm loosening.

"Nick? *Nick*. Don't you dare die on me," I shouted.

The police and paramedics burst into the room and

rushed over. Gabriella put her arm around me and everything moved in slow motion. I subconsciously noted how Nick and Scott's blood had soaked through my jeans, but I didn't care. All I could do was sit there, realization staring me in the face. Scott was dead and Nick laid in a pool of his own blood . . . because of me. It was all my fault.

CHAPTER 2

HADLEY

"You gonna be okay by yourself?" Gabriella asked.

Nodding, I hugged her and Paxton both. "I'll be fine. Thank you for trying to catch the guy who did this. You risked your life," I said to Paxton.

He shrugged. "I just wish I'd caught the fucker. Let us know if there's anything we can do."

I nodded. "I will. But I think you've done more than enough for me at this point. I really can't thank you enough."

They made their way to the door just as my phone started to ring. It was Felicity. Everything had moved so fast, all I could tell her after the accident was that

Nick was in the hospital and that she had to get there. I dreaded having to explain the details.

"Felicity."

"What the hell is going on? What happened to Nick?" she demanded, her voice rough. I could hear squealing tires in the background.

I had cried so much, I didn't think it was possible to shed another tear. My mind was numb and my whole body hurt. "Someone broke into my house and shot Nick and Scott. Scott didn't make it. They told me to run, and . . ." I stopped and threw a hand over my mouth. The guilt came rushing back. I hated myself for putting them in that situation. "They told me to run and I did. Scott would be alive if it wasn't for me. And who knows about Nick," I sobbed.

"It's not your fault. Nick will be okay. We have to believe he'll be okay." We cried together until the police chief, Robert Wilson, cleared his throat.

"Felicity, call me as soon as you find anything out about Nick. I have to go."

We said our goodbyes and I turned to face the chief.

"I know this is a difficult time for you, but I need to ask you some questions," he said. Robert was a middle-aged man with salt and peppered hair and almost a head taller than me, which was pretty tall considering I was five foot ten. I looked up at him and nodded.

"Okay. But I should probably call my dad before

this gets onto the news."

He shook his head. "No need. I called him already."

I squeezed my eyes shut. "Does he know about Scott?"

He sighed and when I opened my eyes, he nodded. "He was a good friend of your father's, just like I am. George and I go way back, Miss Rivers. And with everything that's happened, I have a solution to keep you safe. Now follow me. We have a long night ahead of us."

"You're moving me *where*?" I gasped, shooting to my feet. Robert sat back in his chair while I paced his office.

Before he could respond, my father spoke up first, his deep voice resonating out of the telephone speaker. "I'm sorry, pumpkin. I know this isn't want you want, but we have to keep you safe, at all costs."

"I understand the concern, but why do I have to go all the way to Wyoming? Why can't I stay in California, somewhere closer to home?"

"Because," Robert interrupted, drawing my attention, "we need you in a safe place; where no one will recognize you, and no one would look for you. Even your father isn't going to know exactly where you're going." He leaned forward, his gaze serious. "With that being said, no one can know of your location, not even your friends. Understand? You will be going dark until we catch this bastard."

My gut clenched and I nodded, tears springing to my eyes at the thought of not seeing Nick, or going to Scott's funeral. My mind shifted to Scott's family, and the pain they'd be going through. I wouldn't be around to tell them how sorry I was. Then there was Nick, who was going to be fighting for his life without me to help him through. He'd always been there for me, and now I'd be leaving him in his greatest hour of need.

My dad sighed and the sound startled me. "Not to mention, sweetheart, your tour will have to be put on hold."

I gasped, I'd totally forgotten about my upcoming commitments across the country.

"There's just no other way. Once word gets out to the media, your fans will understand. You'll be too easy of a target if that bastard knows where to find you."

Exhausted, I sat in the seat across from Robert. "When do I leave?"

"Tomorrow morning, once all your papers go through. You'll no longer be Hadley Rivers. We'll have to give you a new identity."

Nodding, I wiped at the tears sliding down my cheek. I would be abandoning everyone I cared about, while they dealt with my mess. "How long will I be gone?"

Robert shrugged. "Hard to say. Obviously, if we don't have luck finding the cocksucker, we can't keep you hidden forever. But you'll just be putting yourself at risk if you come back too soon, and without a plan in place."

"I understand." I couldn't stay away forever, and I definitely didn't want to ever step foot in my house again. The memories were too powerful. I'd never be able to walk in my kitchen and not see Scott and Nick laying in pools of blood. "Where will I be staying tonight? I can't go back home."

"You're coming with me," Robert explained. "My wife already has the guest bedroom ready for you. Deputy Savage is at your house now, grabbing some of your things. It should be enough until you get to Wyoming." He looked down at the phone and cleared his throat. "George, I think that about wraps it up. I'm going to step out so you two can talk."

"Thanks, Robert. I appreciate you taking care of my daughter."

"Anytime." Robert grabbed his keys and stepped out of the room.

As soon as the door clicked shut, I picked up the phone and sat there; the enormity of the situation hitting me all at once.

"Hadley, you there?"

I took a deep breath. "I'm here. I keep thinking I'm going to wake up from this nightmare."

"Don't beat yourself up. It's not your fault."

"Does Scott's family know?" I asked, swallowing hard. He didn't have a wife or kids, but he still had parents and siblings who loved him.

The line grew quiet before he came back on. "Yes. They're upset, but they knew the risks."

"Will you please tell them I'm sorry?"

"Yes, pumpkin, I will. Now why don't you go home with Robert and get some rest. You have a long day tomorrow."

That was an understatement.

CHAPTER 3

BLAKE

"I'm taking Nightshade out for a last minute ride. Is there anything else you need me to do before I go?" Tyla asked. She guided the black stallion out of the stall and hopped into the saddle.

Lifting my hat, I wiped the sweat off my brow. "Nah, you're good. I have a new mare coming tomorrow. I'd like you to work with her as much as you can. The Wright's couldn't handle her, so they're sending her to us."

She snorted. "*Us?*"

"To *you* then, smart ass." I chuckled. "Although, I have to say, I'm just about as good as you now."

Grinning from ear to ear, she pulled her curly,

blonde hair into a ponytail. "So you think. Everyone knows I'm the best."

And she was. Tyla Rand was one of the most talented and hardest working women I'd ever met. She was around my age and wise beyond her years. I'd never seen anyone so experienced with horses. For the past year, she'd been coaching me on how to break them, just like my grandfather had done for a living. I wanted to live up to his legacy.

I scratched behind Nightshade's ear and glanced up at her. "Go, before it gets too late. I'll meet you and the guys at the bar."

She winked. "Got it, boss. You might want to steer clear of Singleton though. I think he knows about you and Rayna. He was looking for you the other night."

I scoffed. "He knows where to find me. Besides, I'm not scared of that twat. Rayna came onto *me* . . . I simply showed her what it was like to ride a real man." Trent Singleton was an arrogant douche and rodeo cowboy, always causing trouble. I'd been waiting for the day I could kick his ass.

"Okay," she laughed, "but if you fight him, make sure to do it outside the bar. Remember, I'm friends with the owners."

I winked up at her. "You have nothing to worry about."

She shook her head – clearly not believing me – and

took off for the fields. "See ya tonight!" she shouted.

Inside the barn, my phone rang. I rushed in, recognizing the number on the screen. "I'll be damned, if it isn't Robert Wilson," I answered.

Robert chuckled. "What's up, Evans? You enjoying the cowboy life out there?"

I looked at my horses and the snow-capped mountains. Was I enjoying it? Hell yeah, I was. It was hard work, but I couldn't imagine going back to my old life. "You have no idea. I never thought I'd enjoy riding horses and shoveling shit."

"And that is something I never thought I'd hear you say. Have you taken on any missions since you've been out there?"

"A couple small tasks. Why, what's up?"

He cleared his throat. "Just asking."

"And why do I not believe that?"

The line went quiet for a second. "Because it's a lie. I need a damn favor."

"Thought so. I knew you wouldn't call just to shoot the shit. What do you need?"

I sat down on a hay bale and kicked up my feet. The sun had started to go down behind the mountains, bringing in the cool, evening breeze. It was early May and the weather was perfect, not like back home where it was smoldering and humid.

He blew out a heavy sigh. "We had a suspect escape

after a break in. He killed one and the other is in critical condition."

I sat up and held the phone closer. "Any leads on where the suspect went?"

"Not yet. We're working on it."

"Do you need me to find him?"

He chuckled, but there was no humor in it. "If only that were it. I have someone else on it already. What I need from you is something much different."

When he explained the situation, there was only one thing I could say. "Fuck no."

CHAPTER 4

HADLEY

"Hadley," a soft voice called out, followed by a knock.

It was Susan, Robert's wife. She did her best to make me feel at home, but I couldn't find the comfort. She had kind brown eyes and chocolate colored hair, adorned with wisps of gray. Talking to her helped get my mind off of things, but once I was left alone for the night, everything came rushing back.

Rubbing my swollen, red eyes, I left my perch on the window seat and opened the door. Still in her flannel pajamas, she held out a tray with a stack of pancakes and syrup. My stomach growled at the smell.

Her smile vanished the moment she looked at my

face. "Oh dear, have you been in here crying all night?" Walking past me, she set the tray down on the dresser and turned a motherly glare my way, propping her hands on her hips.

Surely, I didn't look that bad? I glanced at myself in the full length mirror, and saw I was worse than I thought. "I was thinking about Scott and Nick. My heart hurts for them."

She glanced over at the perfectly made bed, her expression weary. "You didn't sleep either?"

I shrugged. "I was afraid I'd have nightmares."

Her face and arms relaxed. Reaching for me, her warm fingers grasped my wrists. "I know this isn't easy for you, but you need to take care of yourself. You're leaving for Wyoming in just a couple of hours. Why don't you eat and take a shower? I'll be downstairs if you want to talk."

My throat closed up, so I nodded, hoping it'd appease her. Once she was gone, I ate as much as I could, then took a long, hot shower. The deputy who'd packed my bag of clothes put several pairs of jeans and T-shirts inside. I grabbed whatever came first and put them on. Before I could leave the room, my phone rang and I jumped. It was a number I didn't recognize.

"Hello?"

"Hadley, it's me," Felicity rasped. My heart dropped; she sounded horrible.

Clenching the phone, I collapsed onto the bed. "Please tell me you have good news."

She sniffled. "Not exactly. Nick's been put in a medical coma. He went through several surgeries last night to repair the damage. They . . ." Her voice caught and she sucked in a shaky breath. "They lost him at one point and had to revive him."

I slapped a hand to my mouth. "Oh my God."

"All we can do is pray."

Squeezing my eyes shut, I choked back tears. "I will, every day." I glanced at the clock and realized I only had a little time before my plane left for Wyoming. Grabbing my bag, I got to my feet, decision made. "I'm coming out there. I have to see him."

"Are you sure you're able to? What happened after I left?"

I blew out a frustrated breath. "It's a long story. I'll explain when I get there."

"Okay. Just be careful. The pariahs are everywhere."

"Noted. I'll be there as soon as I can." Before hanging up, she told me the room number and I said my goodbyes.

We always called the paparazzi, the pariahs. It didn't surprise me they were hanging around the hospital. Some of them were really nice, but most couldn't wait to catch you with your pants down so they could screw you in the ass. Anything to get a headline.

Opening the bedroom door, I took one last look around before heading downstairs. I froze on the steps when the front door slammed shut and a voice I'd never heard before echoed throughout the house. My heart stopped and I sucked in a breath. Had the creeper found me already?

As soon as Robert laughed, I breathed a sigh of relief. It was then I realized how afraid I'd become. Whoever broke into my house was after *me*. What if he was never caught? I'd never feel safe again.

Turning the corner, I spotted Robert in the kitchen with another man. He was tall, closer to my age, with blond hair and the muscular build of a fighter. His blue gaze met mine and he acknowledged me with a smile. He cleared his throat and Robert turned around to address me.

"Good morning. Did you sleep well?"

"Do you want the truth, or a polite lie?"

He chuckled. "I'll take that as a no." Motioning toward his friend, he said, "Hadley, I'd like you to meet Logan Chandler. He's a good friend of mine and the one who'll be escorting you to the great state of Wyoming."

I held out my hand. "Nice to meet you, Logan."

He shook my hand and winked. "Likewise."

"Are you going to be ready to leave for the airport in an hour?" Robert asked.

Susan handed me a cup of coffee and patted my

shoulder before leaving the room. I set my bag down and took a giant gulp; it burned going down, but my body was numb. "Actually, on the way there, I need to stop by the hospital to see Nick."

Robert sighed. "That's not possible."

My head jerked up and I glared at him. "Why not?"

"Because you need to stay hidden. The hospital is swarming with every fucking news station and gossip rag in the city; all waiting for you to show up." He stepped back and leaned against the bar with his arms crossed, trying his best to look intimidating in his Minions pajama pants—it wasn't working. He had a point, sure, but I couldn't let him stand in my way.

I set my cup down. "There has to be something we can do. I'm not leaving town without seeing him."

Robert and Logan looked at each other, but it was Logan who turned to me and spoke. "There is a way, but you're probably not going to like it."

I stood up straight. "I'll do anything. Let's go."

A small smile splayed across his face. "Your wish is my command."

When Logan said he had a way in, I didn't realize it was going to be traveling at breakneck speeds through rush hour traffic on a sport bike. Whizzing by vehicles at ninety miles an hour, I screamed a few times and kept my eyes shut. My teeth ached from clenching so hard, but I sucked it up and held on until we got to the hospital.

"You can let me go now, Hadley." Logan chuckled, pulling off his helmet. When I didn't let go, he squeezed my hands, still tightly wrapped around his waist. My muscles shook from holding him so hard.

I slowly pried my hands apart and slid off the bike. "Sorry. I've never been on a motorcycle before. At least the paparazzi didn't recognize us when we pulled in. I mean, how could they when we were going at light speed?" I started to unbuckle my helmet but he grabbed my hands, pulling me to him.

"Keep it on. We're not alone out here. Pretend to fumble with the straps until we get in the elevator." I nodded and followed along beside him. There were a few people in the parking garage, but luckily, we were able to get in the elevator by ourselves. Once inside, he helped me with the helmet and pulled it off.

"Here, put this on," he said, handing me a baseball cap from his back pocket. "We don't want anyone recognizing you."

I snorted and slid it down on my head. "I doubt they could anyway. I look like death."

The elevator doors opened and we stepped out. I already knew where to go. My heart sped up the closer we got to Nick's room.

A voice called out. "Hadley?"

I gasped and jerked around. Tristan Abernathy stood in the doorway of the waiting room with the rest of the hockey team spread out behind him, dressed in their jerseys and lounging in chairs. Tristan looked worse than any of them. His dirty blond hair was unkempt and he looked exhausted.

"Tristan," I breathed.

"Where have you been? We were all worried about you."

I wrapped my arms around his neck. "I'm in protective custody. I'm not supposed to be here, but I had to see Nick."

He held me close, burying his face in my hair. His chest shook and it broke my heart. "He doesn't look good, Hads. What if he doesn't make it?"

"We have to believe he will." Once he let me go, Kip and Dawson, two of my favorites on the hockey team, stole me away and I threw an arm around them both. They were twins, both with dark brown hair and blue eyes. "I'm going to miss you guys so much."

"We're not going anywhere, sweetheart," Kip assured me.

Swallowing hard, I stepped back. "But I am, and I don't know when I'll be back."

"Where are you going?" Tristan asked, placing a

hand on my shoulder. I glanced over at Logan, who shook his head.

"I can't say," I said, looking up at Tristan. "It's for my protection."

"When will you be back?"

I shrugged. "I don't know."

"We're running out of time, Hadley," Logan called.

Nodding once, I walked to the door and then faced the team. "Good luck at the games, guys. I won't physically be there, but know I'll be watching." I hugged Tristan one more time. "I'll find a way to keep in touch, okay? I'm hoping they'll catch this bastard soon, so I can come home."

Logan walked with me to the end of the hall, to Nick's closed door. Taking a deep breath, I held onto the doorknob, afraid of what I'd see on the other side. I closed my eyes and felt warm tears fall down my cheeks.

"You have five minutes," Logan murmured.

I blew out a breath and opened the door, letting it shut quietly behind me. The TV was on, but I could barely hear the sound from the pounding in my ears. Felicity was asleep in the corner, a box of tissues on her lap, snoring lightly. The curtain blocked Nick from sight. Taking a few steps into the room, he came into view and I covered my eyes with my hands. He was so pale and definitely didn't look like the vibrant jokester I knew him to be.

Taking a moment to collect myself, I breathed deep and made my way to the bed. "Nick?" I whispered, clasping my fingers gently through his. I thought I'd get a response, but there was nothing. He was so still. My heart broke, and I hated myself more than ever. I'd lost Scott and there was a possibility I'd lose him too . . . all of this because of me, for *my* protection.

What would I do without him?

"I'm sorry, Nick. I'm so, so sorry. I'd give anything to take back time." I held his hand to my face, my tears soaking his skin.

"You're here," Felicity said.

I glanced over my shoulder. "Hey. Sorry for waking you. I can't stay long, but I had to stop by."

She slowly got to her feet and a handful of used tissues fell to the floor. I hated having to leave her. "Do you have to go back to the station?" she asked.

I turned my focus back to Nick, swallowing the large lump in my throat. I had to tell her the truth. "No. I have to go away for awhile. I didn't want to tell you over the phone."

"Where are you going?"

A light tap sounded on the door and when it opened, Logan stuck his head in. He nodded at Felicity and then focused on me. "We have to go."

I lifted my finger. "Just one more minute." As soon as the door shut, my chest hurt. I hated goodbyes.

"What's going on, Hadley?" Felicity demanded.

Reluctantly, I let Nick's hand go and faced her. "I'm under police protection, until they can find whoever did this. In the meantime, I'll have to cancel my shows. You don't have to worry about any of the details. I'll get it handled. Soon, Nick will be up and moving around and we can get back to work. This whole nightmare will be over."

Lip quivering, she lowered her head and nodded. "As much as I hate you leaving, I understand. I just know Nick will be worried sick about you when he wakes up."

My time was running out, so I hugged her quick. "I'll call and check up on you both every day. Just make sure to answer your phone. The number will probably be untraceable."

"I will." She stepped aside so I could move closer to Nick.

I kissed his cheek and rested my forehead against his. "Come back to us. I miss you already." One of my tears fell on his cheek, and I wiped it away.

"How long do you think you'll be gone?" Felicity wondered.

"I don't know," I whispered, turning to face her. "I honestly don't know."

CHAPTER 5

BLAKE

"How's your hand?" Tyla asked, smirking at the gashes on my knuckles. "You really messed Trent's shit up last night."

I grabbed Snowflake's brush and glided it down her body. My hands hurt like a bitch, but I'd do it all over again just to hear the crunch of Singleton's nose as I pounded on his face. His first mistake was seeking me out.

Clenching my fist, I watched the blood ooze out of the gash on my right hand. "It's fine. Can't say the same for Singleton's face though."

She snorted. "That's for damn sure. I don't think he'll be messing with you for a while. Did Rayna come over to nurse you back to health?"

I moved over to Snowflake's other side, brushing her gently. "She tried, but I'm done with that thundercunt. I don't need the drama."

"It's not like you can't find someone else. Every female in town's been salivating over you since you moved here."

"Including you?" I joked.

"Please," she scoffed with a roll of her eyes. "You were intriguing for like a second, then reality struck. You're not my type."

We both laughed and finished grooming the young mare. Tyla was a beautiful woman, but I knew better than to get involved with someone I worked with. I'd learned that hard lesson long ago.

"I think this little beauty is going to be one hell of a horse," Tyla said proudly.

"That she is. She's looking good. In fact, I'll be taking over her training tomorrow."

Her eyes went wide. "You sure you can handle that?" All morning she'd been working with Snowflake to tame her down. There was a lot of work still to be done, but I had no doubt we could do it. Before I could reply, her phone rang. She waltzed off to answer it while I stayed with Snowflake.

The wild little beast bumped my hand with her muzzle and snorted. Chuckling, I scratched behind her ear. "You gonna be a good girl for me tomorrow? Josie wants to ride you someday and I have to make sure you're not going to throw her off." Josie Wright was eight years old and an amazing young rider. Unfortunately, when her parents bought Snowflake, she turned out to be a little too much to handle.

"As much as she likes you, I'd say you'll get her tamed in no time," Tyla claimed. Her smile faded as she slipped her phone into her back pocket.

"What's wrong?" I asked.

"I need to go out of town for a couple of weeks. I know it's short notice, but it's something I really need to do."

"Is everything okay?"

"I hope so. I'll know more once I get to California. Can you handle this one without me?" she asked, nodding toward Snowflake.

Snowflake bumped me again and I laughed. "I think she likes me better than you anyway. Now get the hell out of here, I have work to do."

Brows furrowed, she studied me, no doubt wondering if I'd be okay without her expertise. "All right, I'm leaving. I'll call you when I'm coming back into town. And you know Ryker is always around the corner if you need help with anything."

I pointed to her car and chuckled. "Go already. There's no need to worry about me."

As much as her help was needed, I wasn't going to make her think she had to stay. She waved at me as she backed out and took off down the long driveway, a cloud of dust following in her wake.

My grandfather had handled the ranch on his own for years. I could do the same. He specialized more in training horses, than herding cattle, but I liked doing both.

After closing up the barn, I started for the house. The sound of gravel crunched in the distance, and at first, I thought it was Tyla coming back, but it wasn't her car. It was a black SUV with tinted windows. Lifting my hat, I wiped the sweat off my brow and lowered it back down. If it was Singleton, he was stupider than I thought.

Body tense, I was prepared to fight. However, when the car door opened, I couldn't help but grin. "You've got to be shitting me. What the hell are you doing here?"

Logan Chandler, a good friend of mine and one of the best undercover agents I knew, waltzed toward me with the biggest smile on his face. "I can't believe what I'm seeing," he joked, extending his hand. "Please tell me you haven't turned Brokeback on me?"

"Fuck no. You know me better than that."

We shook hands and he chuckled. "You're right. Last I recall, you had a new piece of ass every week, especially after things ended with Brooklyn."

"That was a long time ago, brother," I said, slapping him on the shoulder. Brooklyn was the only serious relationship I'd ever had. I loved her, but fucked it all up. Now she was gone and happy with someone else. I hadn't talked to her in almost a year. "So what brings you all the way out to BFE? You're not the type to make house calls."

Releasing a heavy sigh, he glanced back at the car, then to me. "Can we go inside and talk? I could use a beer about now."

I focused on the car, but couldn't see anyone. "Who's in there, Chandler?"

"It's a long story, which is why I need the beer." He followed me inside and I grabbed us both a beer out of the refrigerator. Once he guzzled his down, he looked out at the car again, biting his lip. "Whatever you do, don't kill me."

I lifted the bottle to my mouth and froze. "Fuck me. What did you do?"

He turned around, smile gone. "I brought you something, or better yet . . . someone."

It didn't take long for everything to fall into place. I should've known. Slamming my beer down, I pointed angrily at the car. "Take Miss Hollywood back. I don't want her here."

Logan lifted his hands and stepped back. "Why won't you take this job? You're the only one trusted and available to keep her safe."

"Bullshit! What about you? You fucking take her."

He shook his head. "I'm leaving on another mission tomorrow. Anyway, you're the one Robert wants. Hadley's dad is one of the richest men in the country and he's willing to pay big money for your services."

"I don't want his goddamn money."

"You sure about that? Think about what you could do to this place if you had ten million laying around," he replied.

My eyes bulged. "You're shitting me."

"Nope. And trust me, I'd guard her body for next to nothing. She's hot as hell."

"Looks aren't everything. She's Hollywood, and this," I said, gesturing to my farmhouse, "ain't exactly the Ritz-Carlton. Her kind won't fit in here."

Logan shrugged a shoulder. "You'd be surprised. She's not as bad as you make her sound."

Clenching my teeth, I stormed to the window. "I'm not going to be her servant, and she won't find any maids here. I'll keep her safe, but that's it. I won't be at her beck and call. If she wants to stay, she has to live by my rules. Got it?"

He joined me by the window. "Don't be so hard on her, Evans. Her bodyguard was just killed and her boyfriend is in critical condition. She's in a bad place right now."

"Since when did you turn soft?" I grumbled.

"She has that effect on people. You'll see what I mean."

I scoffed. "Just make sure her father pays up."

He patted me on the shoulder. "He's good for it. Once he hears from me, he'll give you a call to transfer the money."

"Good," I said, crossing my arms over my chest.

"Do you want me to bring her in and introduce her? I have to get back to the airport."

"Might as well," I grumbled.

Logan marched out of the kitchen and to the car. The second Hadley stepped out and I saw her face, I knew I was in trouble.

CHAPTER 6

HADLEY

"What took you so long? You had me worried," I said.

Logan shut the door and grabbed my bag out of the back. "Sorry about that. It took longer than I thought."

"Is everything okay?"

Shouldering my bag, he sighed, looking down at me with troubled blue eyes. "You're not in California anymore, Hadley. Things are different here. You're going to have to adapt to this lifestyle so you fit in. People are going to look at you and think they see Hadley, but you're not her anymore. Understand?"

I nodded. "I know. My name is Anna Sawyer and I'm a twenty-five-year-old real estate agent from

North Carolina. Blake Evans is my stepbrother and I'm visiting because I just got divorced from my husband and I needed to get as far away from home as I could." I paused and took a deep breath. "I took drama in high school. I'm pretty sure I can pull it off."

He smiled. "Good. I think you're all set. I put your ID's and an untraceable cell phone in your bag, along with my number. You can call me anytime."

I followed him to the front door and stepped inside. The house had a warm feel to it, all western-like, with deer and buffalo heads on the wall. It was just like being on the set of a cowboy movie. I half expected John Wayne to mosey around the corner at any minute.

I gazed around in awe. "This is amazing."

"So it meets your standards?" an abrasive voice called out.

Gasping, I jerked around and found the owner of the voice glaring at me. For a second I lost my ability to speak. His brown hair was damp with sweat and he was covered in streaks of dirt on his tanned, bare chest. He was gorgeous; except for the scowl on his face. Why was he looking at me like that? Surely that wasn't Blake.

Huffing, Logan put his arm protectively around my shoulder, speaking through clenched teeth. "Hadley, I'd like you to meet dickface. Crap, I'm sorry . . . I meant Blake. I got a little confused there." Body tense, Blake rolled his eyes and my stomach dropped. He did *not* want me there. "Blake, this is Hadley," Logan continued, squeezing my shoulder. "She'll be your guest for the next few weeks."

Blake pointed to the stairs. "Your room is up there, first door on the left. I don't have servants, so if you want something, get it yourself."

I held up my hands. "I don't have servants." Unfortunately, he'd already turned on his heel and stalked away. Huffing, I glared up at Logan. "I can't believe you're leaving me here. Why is he acting like that?"

He set my bag down. "Want the truth?" I nodded. "Basically, he thinks you're going to be an uppity cunt. What he doesn't know is that you're actually a down to earth person. He'll come around once he gets to know you."

"Why can't I stay with you? You can keep me safe."

"I would if I could, but I'm leaving for another mission as soon as I leave here. You'll be fine. You're a strong-willed woman." Leaning in close, he whispered in my ear. "Just don't take shit from him. Show Blake you can handle this and he'll turn around."

As much as I wanted to believe I could, I doubted myself. I didn't belong here and it was evident. "Okay," I whispered, "I can do this."

Logan led me upstairs to my room and set my bag on the bed. The room was all white and elegant, clearly a female's room. It was beautiful; definitely a contrast to the masculinity downstairs.

"I have to go now. Remember, you can call me anytime."

My eyes burned, but I refused to cry. All I wanted was to be back at home and have Scott still alive. Maybe that was why I liked Logan so much; he reminded me of a younger version of him. Opening my arms, I rushed over to him, wrapping them around his neck. "Thank you for watching over me. Be safe on your mission."

He squeezed me tight and let go. "I will. If I need to come back and kick shitdick's ass, just let me know."

The thought made me smile. I wished he would preemptively do it. Maybe then, Blake wouldn't be such a prick. "You've got it."

Turning on his heel, his footsteps echoed off the wooden stairs, and all too quickly, he was out the front door. I didn't watch him leave because I knew I'd be tempted to chase after him and jump in the car. If Blake didn't want me there, why did he agree to let me stay in the first place?

The house was quiet, but there was a noise coming from the back. Logan told me not to take any shit and I wasn't planning on it. Blake was going to talk to me, even if I had to force it out of him. Finding my way through the huge house, I stormed outside. With his back to me and a hammer in his hands, Blake crouched low to the ground, pounding nails into a wooden fence. His muscles flexed with each strike, but I was too pissed off to even notice how sexy his body was. *Who am I kidding?* I noticed the first time I saw him.

"Dammit," I hissed low. I couldn't be thinking about him like that. He was an ass, end of story.

Getting to his feet, he glanced at me, then focused back on the task at hand. "Something I can help you with?" he muttered.

"I thought maybe, since we're going to be stuck with each other for a while, we could talk. Our stories need to be consistent if we go out in public. I don't know what all you know." I said it nice and sweet, even though I wanted to take his hammer and slam it against his head.

He turned to me. "That's the thing, Hollywood. I don't know our story because I didn't want to take this fucking job. Just know this, I'm not going to kiss your ass because you're famous."

Sucking in a breath, I could feel the blood rushing to my face.

"You see me as a dirty, worthless cowboy who doesn't know anything other than shoveling shit and playing in the dirt." He stepped closer and I stumbled back, the look in his eyes making me tremble. "I'm a trained killer, princess. The government calls me in to solve cases they can't. But yet, here I am . . . babysitting *you*. It's a fucking joke."

My heart raced, anger boiling in my veins. "So keeping me safe is a joke? I'm here because Robert says you're the best." I laughed with no humor behind it. "I find myself wanting to explain who I am, but then I remember I don't give a shit what you think of me. I didn't want to leave my family and friends behind, believe me. If you want me gone, I'll be glad to go. I refuse to be treated like shit when none of this was my fault."

He studied me for a minute. A small smile appeared, making me shiver. "Actually, I don't think I want you to go," he said.

I crossed my arms over my chest. "Oh yeah? Why is that?"

His grin grew wider. "I'm starting to think you might be good to have around. How about we trade services? I keep you safe, in return for a favor."

"I'm *not* sleeping with you."

He shook his head. "And there you go, assuming shit. I don't need you to get a piece of ass, sweetheart. I can get that anywhere."

"You probably do, too." I grimaced. "Look, I don't exactly need you either."

"Great. Now that we have that settled, let's get down to business. If you want me to keep you safe, you have to work for it. Chores around the ranch will do fine. However," he started, glancing down at my manicured hands, "I don't think those will stay pretty very long."

I clenched my fists, hiding my long, pink nails. "Why don't you just worry about keeping me safe and I'll do what I have to do."

With a devilish smirk, he looked into my eyes. I stared right back and didn't waver. "You think you can handle the job?" he asked, his voice seductive and deep.

I stood up straighter. "I know I can. Just tell me what to do." I wasn't going to let him mock me.

"All right. Be up and ready to go at dawn. Let's see what you're made of."

CHAPTER 7

BLAKE

"Good morning, Mr. Evans," Jerrod said, handing me a thermos.

I opened it up and took a deep breath. "Is this the coffee you were telling me about?"

He smiled wide. "Yep. My mom said you wanted to try it. My grandmother in Hawaii sends it to us. Supposedly, it's the best."

I took a sip. "I believe you're right. Will you tell your mother thank you?"

He nodded. "Of course. She had to go in early to the hotel, but I'll tell her this afternoon."

Jerrod Kalani was fifteen years old and a hard worker. His mother had wanted me to hire him to keep him out of trouble. When he'd found out I was a cop, he got his act together quickly. It was fun telling him stories of my adventures undercover. I couldn't wait to get back in that line of work again. Keeping the ranch up had taken me away from it all.

Jerrod started toward Snowflake's stall. "Wait," I called.

He turned around, furrowing his brows. "Is there something else you need me to do first? I have to make sure I get to school early so I can finish studying for my Algebra test." Every morning, he'd come and help me in the barn, before getting ready for school. I never asked him to do it, but it was something he enjoyed. Plus, he got paid nicely for it.

I couldn't help but smile. "Why don't you go and study, instead of worrying about this today. I got it covered."

"Are you sure?"

"Go." I chuckled, waving him off. "And good luck on your test. I'll see you tomorrow morning."

"Thanks." He rushed to his bike and sped down the driveway. As soon as he was gone, the light in Hadley's room turned on. I could see her silhouette through the sheer, white curtains.

I had to hand it to her, she knew how to fight back. For dinner last night, I'd placed a can of beans on the kitchen counter with a note that read, *Enjoy*. It was meant as a joke, but she'd opened them up and ate straight out of the can. I was impressed. For the rest of the night, I didn't hear any more from her, other than the sound of her crying softly in her room. It made me feel like shit for being a dick to her.

It wasn't long before the back door slammed against the side of the house. Judging by the sun peeking behind the mountains, she was right on time.

"I'm here," she called out.

Over my shoulder, I watched her approach. She had on a pair of ripped jeans and a snug green T-shirt that hugged her body perfectly. *Fuck, she's hot.* It didn't help that I could see her nipples through her shirt. My cock twitched, but thankfully, I had my back to her. Snowflake whinnied and stomped her hoof. I guided her out of the stall and Hadley's eyes brightened.

"She's beautiful," she gushed. Reaching her hand out, she ran it down Snowflake's face.

"Being a city girl and all, I didn't think you'd like animals."

Her gaze darkened. "You're going to start this again?"

"What? All I said was, I didn't think you'd like animals."

She rolled her eyes. "And I guess I can't sing country music because I'm from the city too, right? You can't always judge a person by where they're from. Obviously, you were raised in a barn, but I'm not holding that against you. Now where do you want me?"

She was a spitfire; I liked it. It took all I had not to laugh, especially when I pointed at the rake. "Snowflake's stall needs to be cleaned out. You can take her shit and put it in the dump truck over there," I said, pointing to the old truck. The look on her face absolutely priceless.

"So it's literally a *dump* truck?"

"Yep. And once that's done, I'll need you to clean out the rest of the stalls. Think you can handle it?"

Sucking in a breath, she blew it out and headed straight for the rake without acknowledging my question. Out of the corner of my eye, I watched her slip into the stall and get to work. I would've given anything to take a picture. She looked like she'd blow chunks at any moment.

While she finished up the stall, I went about my morning workout with Snowflake and moved on to Nightshade, my black stallion. My grandfather had bought him for me a couple of years before he died, hoping we'd be a good match for each other. He was strong and fast, perfect for rounding up cattle.

After I finished my chores for the day, I sat on a hay bale and watched Hadley finish up in the barn. My hat sat low over my eyes, as if I was snoozing. She glared and flipped me off a few times, but I kept a straight face. When she was done, she stormed over to me and hit my boots with the rake.

"I'm done cleaning the stalls. What's next?"

Taking a deep breath, I scrunched my nose. "I think you need to take a shower. You smell like shit."

She turned on her heel and grumbled the word 'asshole' under her breath. I burst out laughing and followed closely behind her. When she got inside, she quickly rushed upstairs and slammed the bedroom door. I wondered how long it would take her to break.

CHAPTER 8

HADLEY
(One Week Later)

Blake was a fucking prick. There was no way I could survive being with him for months. Hell, just a week with him was torture. The physical labor I could handle, but the mental jabs would be my downfall. I needed support more than anything and I wasn't going to get it from him.

Luckily, I had the phone Logan left me. I needed to hear Felicity's voice. She answered on the second ring.

"Hello?"

I cleared my throat. "It's me."

"Oh my God, Hadley, you sound horrible. Are you okay?"

"Trying to be. It's been a long day. How's Nick?"

She blew out a frustrated breath. "Still the same. He hasn't woken up yet. You wanna talk to him?"

A tear slid down my cheek. "Yes."

The phone shuffled and I heard her voice in the background. "He's on."

"Hey Nick, it's me. I wish I could be there with you. I miss you and Felicity so much. When you pull through this, we're going to celebrate, okay? It sucks not being able to hear your voice. I could use it right about now." The line grew quiet and Felicity got back on.

"How's it going out there?" she asked.

I had just gotten out of the shower and my arms were on fire from shoveling all day. All I'd had to eat were a bowl of carrots and a cucumber. "It's horrible," I answered honestly. "The guy they have me with is a complete douche. I've tried to be nice, but he's still an ass."

"What have you been doing?"

I snorted in disgust. "You don't want to know. Let's just say I hate the guy I'm with more than I hate Lydia Turner."

"Wow," she gasped. "That's pretty bad."

Lydia was my nemesis and it was no secret we had bad blood. When I started winning more awards than her, she openly trash talked me to the media. The paparazzi had tried to get me to retaliate, but I refused to fuel the fire.

"It's worse than bad," I stated.

"I'm sorry, Hadley. I know it can't be easy. In other news, I did spend today going over your schedule. I know you said you were going to handle it, but I went ahead and canceled your shows. Everyone's talking about you right now."

I sat down on the bed. "Great. I can only imagine what they're saying."

"Just do me a favor and stay away from the TV. Can you do that?"

"Shouldn't be a problem. I don't even have time to watch TV anyway." The line went quiet and all I could hear were the beeping of machines and the sound of Felicity's breathing. She had to be exhausted. "Felicity?"

"Hmm?"

"I'll call you tomorrow, okay? Thank you for handling my schedule. I promise I was going to do it."

"I know, but I needed something to take my mind off of Nick. I'll talk to you later." We said our goodbyes and hung up.

I didn't want to leave my room, but I was starving. There were no smells coming from the kitchen, which only made me hungrier. A can of beans wasn't going to cut it tonight. The only reason I ate them all week was to prove a point. I wouldn't do that every day.

My dirty clothes really did smell like horse shit,

so I piled them in the laundry basket and took them downstairs. The laundry room was right by the kitchen. I started up a load, then made my way into the kitchen. My cheeks flamed when I saw what was on the counter.

"You have got to be kidding me," I snarled. There was a bottle of water and a pack of beef jerky. I could see Blake through the window with that smug grin of his, but the asshole didn't know I was watching. He rode off on the black horse and disappeared across the pasture. "Payback's a bitch."

I searched through his refrigerator and cabinets until I found everything I needed. It wasn't going to be much of a dinner, but at least it would be hot and substantial. I was starved, so anything I could cook up would be heaven, even if it was eggs, bacon, and frozen biscuits. Ever since I was a kid, I loved breakfast for dinner.

As quick as I could, I whipped up the eggs and bacon and threw the biscuits in the oven. He might think I'm Hollywood and not be able to wipe my own ass, but I was going to show him. Once everything was done, I put everything on my plate and ate it all. I'd never eaten so much in my life. I was down to my last piece of bacon when he waltzed through the door.

"Damn, something smells good in here," he announced.

"Have a nice ride?" I asked, turning to face him. Why did he always have to have his shirt off? It was distracting, making it hard to hate him when he looked like that.

He took off his cowboy hat and strolled over to the stove. "You didn't cook me any?" he asked.

I held up the last bite of bacon and tossed it in my mouth. "I did, but I ate it all. Here," I tossed him the bag of jerky, "bon appetite." Not waiting for him to speak, I turned and walked back to my room. But I did catch the look on his face. Absolutely priceless.

The next morning, I went right out to the barn. Blake was already out there with Snowflake, so I grabbed the rake and went straight to her stall. I gagged a few times from the stench, but after smelling it all morning, I got used to it. I may not have been raised on a ranch, but I was pretty damn good at adapting.

The day went by slow but once Blake was done with the horses, he lounged out on the hay bales and fell asleep. What the hell was with that? Gritting my teeth, I finished cleaning the stalls. "Have you heard anything from Robert?" I asked, raising my voice with each word.

He tilted his hat and acknowledged me before lowering it back over his eyes. "Nope. He'll call when they find something."

I slammed the rake against the wall and started

toward the house. "All right, well I'm done here. I'm going inside."

Jumping off the hay bale, he rushed up behind me. "Hold up, princess, there's something else I need you to do."

"Seriously?" I scoffed. "I've been shoveling your horse shit all day. I might be in hiding, but I still have a job to do."

He motioned for me to follow him. "Like what?"

Rolling my eyes, I followed behind him. "My songs don't write themselves. As soon as I get back home, I'm going to be expected to have some songs to record. Being knee-deep in shit doesn't exactly give me inspiration."

He glanced over his shoulder. "You write your own songs?"

"Shocked?" I countered.

We walked inside and past the staircase. "A little. I thought most of the singers out there only sang shit other people wrote for them."

"Just goes to show how ignorant you are."

He let the comment go and led me into a bedroom where clothes were scattered all over the floor and the bed was unmade. Mouth gaping, I stepped over one of the mounds of dirty clothes.

"Uh, what are we doing in here?"

The room smelled exactly like him, all done up in earthy tones; very cowboyish, with fur-skinned rugs on the floor. There were plaques on the wall, but I couldn't see what they said. Maybe they were given to him for being Douchebag of the Year. Even on the fireplace mantle there were pictures of him and other people, including one with him and a young woman. I wondered who she was.

He waved toward the mess, grabbing my attention. "I need you to clean all this up. I have a date tonight and I don't want her seeing it like this."

"You're joking, right?"

Lifting his shirt, he tossed it on the dirty mound of clothes and started unbuttoning his jeans. "Not at all, princess. You need to hurry before she gets here. I don't think she'll like seeing another woman in my room." Turning his back to me, he lowered his jeans and boxers to the floor, and grabbed the towel that was on his bed, wrapping it around his waist.

I didn't see his backside because I was blinded by anger. As he turned back around, I picked up an armful of his dirty clothes, and hurled them at him as hard as I could. His hands lifted, making him lose his grip on the towel. "Clean up your own damn room, asshole! I'm out of here."

Storming out the door, I rushed upstairs and packed my bag.

"Hadley, *wait*," Blake shouted. He raced up the stairs, but I locked the door before he could get in. As fast as I could, I searched through the phone until I found the number for a cab service. Blake knocked on the door, his voice softer. "Please open up, so we can talk."

Dialing the number, I flipped him off even though he couldn't see me. "Go fuck yourself. It's too late for that."

I requested the cab and hung up quickly. The sooner I could get out of that house, the better. Once I was all packed, I stood by the window until I could see the cab coming down the driveway. Throwing my bag over my shoulder, I slammed open the door. Blake's head jerked up and he lifted his hands in defeat. At least he'd had the decency to put his pants back on.

"Don't go," he said. "Let me explain."

Huffing, I pushed past him and rushed down the stairs. "I don't want to hear a single thing you have to say. It's obvious you don't want me here. You treat your horses better than you treat me."

"Where the hell are you going to go? You're under my protection."

I stopped at the door and opened it wide, the cab crunching on the gravel as it came to a stop. At this point, I was more exhausted and lonely than angry. Taking a deep breath, I turned around and faced him. "I'm a big girl, Mr. Evans. I can take care of myself. I don't need you to keep me safe. But I have to say, I'm sorely disappointed."

His jaw clenched. "With what?" he asked.

I shrugged. "Robert talked so highly of you, saying you were the best. I guess I didn't expect you to be such an inconsiderate ass." Turning on my heel, I rushed down the driveway and got in the cab.

"Where to, young lady?" the man asked. He was probably the same age as my dad, with white hair and a scruffy beard.

"Anywhere but here. A hotel would be nice."

He put the car into gear. "You got it."

We started down the driveway and when I turned around, Blake was nowhere to be seen; the door was already closed. I thought I was strong enough to put up with him, but I wasn't. Picking up my phone, I dialed Logan's number, hating myself for what I was about to do.

"What's up?" he answered.

I held the phone closer to my ear, whispering low. "I couldn't do it."

"What do you mean?"

"I couldn't stay, Logan. I refuse to listen to Blake's bullshit for another minute. It was a nightmare."

"Jesus Christ, where are you? You shouldn't have left."

"I'll be fine. I'm going to stay at a hotel and figure something out." We entered the city of Jackson Hole and the driver pulled us into a hotel parking lot. The place looked interesting with its dark wood exterior and rustic feel.

"Will this do, Miss?" the driver asked.

"Yes, thanks," I said, handing him a twenty. I got out of the car and he drove away.

Logan cleared his throat. "What hotel are you at?"

"I'm not telling you. You'll go right to Blake. The last thing I need is to deal with him or Robert."

"Who said I was going to call them?"

Rolling my eyes, I strolled toward the door. "It's not like you can't find me anyway. The phone is . . ." Then reality struck. "Fuck me," I growled. It didn't matter where I was, they could always find me as long as I had the phone.

Logan laughed. "Sorry, buttercup. If Evans wants to find you, he can – with or without the phone. It's what he's good at."

I scoffed. "He sure doesn't act like it."

"True, but he really *is* a good guy. I think it would be in your best interest to go back; at least before he finds you."

"Not gonna happen. If he wants me back, he's going to have to drag me, kicking and screaming."

"And he will, sweetheart. I know I would, if you had left me. Maybe you two should pretend to be ex-lovers instead of siblings. I think it works better."

I snorted in disgust. "As long as he keeps his hands to himself." Not to mention, keeping every other part of his body away as well. He was trouble.

CHAPTER 9

BLAKE

"Dude, what the fuck are you doing?" Logan snapped through the phone.

He'd been trying to call me all night, but I'd spent the majority of it going through Hadley's file and researching everything about her on the web, including her NHL star boyfriend. I hadn't bothered to look at her file beforehand, as I'd been too pissed about the assignment. I shouldn't have let my anger cloud my judgment. The more I learned about her, the stupider I felt. Thankfully, her phone acted like a beacon. I would've found her without it anyway. It turned out she picked the hotel Jerrod's mother worked at, so it was easy to reserve the room adjoining hers. The hotels were vacant this time of year.

"Are you even listening to me?" he roared.

I glanced at the picture I had pulled up on my laptop. It was Hadley at the Country Music Awards, holding her award. "It was a mistake," I admitted. "I never should've pushed her as hard as I did."

"You *think*? Why the hell did you fuck with her anyway?"

Sighing, I shut my screen off. "I thought she was going to be a spoiled bitch who needed to be put in her place. I was just testing her."

"And what did you find out?"

I glanced down at her file. "That I'm a fucking idiot."

He chuckled. "You got that right. What are you going to do now? She won't go back without a fight."

In my hand, I held the source of what would prove otherwise. "I beg to differ. By the end of the day, she'll be ready to come back with me. I'm at the hotel."

"Oh hell. What did you do?"

"Let's just say, she's going to be very uncomfortable when she wakes up."

"Good luck, brother. You're gonna need it." We got off the phone and I waited until she left the room before calling the front desk.

"Front desk," Jerrod's mother greeted.

"Hey, Audrey, it's Blake. Has Anna gotten down there yet?" I had to remember to call her Anna instead of Hadley.

"She just walked by," she murmured low. "She's not looking so good. What did you do to her last night? Her skin's all red. If you're trying to get her back, I don't think you went about it the right way."

I held in a chuckle. "Trust me, she'll want to come back home."

"In my day, men would say nice things and take me out to dinner. You could've easily tried that."

"Anna and I don't have that kind of relationship. It's more of a love-hate kind of thing."

She clucked her tongue. "You kids are something else. All right, she's eating breakfast. You're safe to come down."

Instead of going into the restaurant, I grabbed a newspaper and sat in the lounge. I had the perfect view of her, and she looked miserable. Her ball cap rode low over her eyes and she slumped down, as if she didn't want to be seen. She tried not to scratch her bright red skin, covered in large welts. If she ever found out what I did, she would kill me. I didn't realize it would affect her as bad as it did.

She made her way up to the waffle batter dispenser and tried to turn the knob. It didn't budge. Yanking on it a little harder, she screamed out, "Oh my God!" as the lever came off in her hand.

Waffle batter oozed out of the machine onto her

hands and onto the floor. Everyone in the room laughed, especially the kids. Audrey's husband, who also worked maintenance for the hotel, ran inside to help her.

Covered in waffle batter, Hadley rushed out of the restaurant to the elevators. Once she was gone, I helped Bill clean up the mess, knowing she was going to be up in her room for a while.

"I think you guys need a new batter machine." I laughed.

Bill snorted. "Tell me about it. This is the fifth time this year I've had to clean this mess up."

I helped him as much as I could and then retreated to the stairs. Instead of knocking on Hadley's door, I went into my room and unlocked the adjoining one, opening it carefully. Hadley was by the bed, slipping a clean T-shirt over her head. Not only were there hives on her arms, but they were on her back and legs too.

"I see you've had a rough time," I called out, feeling like complete and utter shit.

"Jesus," she squealed, jerking around. She held a hand to her chest, but then relaxed. "I knew I'd be hearing your smartass mouth sooner than later."

I smiled. "So that's why you don't look shocked to see me."

"I knew you could track me," she said, holding up the phone.

"Nice work downstairs, by the way. What did the

waffle maker ever do to you?" I thought it would make her laugh, but she turned away.

"Don't remind me." Huffing, she zipped up her bag. "I'm glad no one knows who I am. I felt like an idiot with everyone laughing at me."

"Well, it *was* kind of funny." She got quiet and started scratching her skin. "Are you okay?"

"Yep."

"Yeah, sure. You just look like a lobster, no biggie. Come on, let's get out of here. You're obviously allergic to something."

Glaring at me, she crossed her arms over her chest. "You expect me to go with you after you were such an ass to me? Speaking of which, how was your date last night?"

"There was no date, Hadley. I was just doing it to get a rise out of you. The same with the barn stalls. You really impressed me though."

She stood up straighter, eyes narrowed. "Glad I could amuse you."

"So . . . what do you say? Are you going to come willingly, or do I need to tie you up?"

Her lips pursed. "Knowing you, you'd like that too much. I'll go willingly."

She was right, I would've tied her up in a heartbeat, and loved every minute of it. She grabbed her bag, but I slipped it off her shoulder as she walked past. I thought she'd fight me on it, but she let it go.

"What changed? Why are you playing nice all of a sudden?"

Opening the room door, I held it so she could walk out. "I did some research last night. Let's just say, I misjudged you."

"Is this your way of apologizing?" she asked, strutting out the door.

"If I say yes, does that mean you'll forgive me?"

She shrugged. "Probably not."

I followed behind her down the hall, and Audrey winked at me as we walked past the front desk. With a smug smile, Hadley got in my truck and I caught the door before she could shut it. I knew that look on her face; it was the same look every woman got when they wanted to fuck something up. "You're going to pay me back, aren't you?"

Her grin grew wider. "You have no idea."

Fuck, I was in trouble.

CHAPTER 10

HADLEY

My skin was on fire. It took all I had not to complain, but dammit to hell, I was miserable. The last thing I wanted was to give Blake a reason to tease me. However, something had changed in him. His whole tone was different, nicer even.

"Do me a favor and stay here. I'll be right back." He parked in front of a doctor's office and shut off the truck.

"What are we doing here?"

"Lock the doors when I leave." Once he was out, I locked the doors and watched him disappear into the entrance.

"Stop looking at him, Hadley. It'll only get you into trouble," I mumbled.

I hated it already, but he was the perfect muse for my new song: bad boy, sexy, gray eyes, and jeans wearing cowboy. In my song, the female was going to tame the wild beast, but I highly doubted anyone could tame Blake. I was sure the hundreds of women who'd ridden him in the past had tried and failed.

Since Blake was still inside, I pulled out my phone and dialed Felicity's number.

"Hey," she answered.

"Hey, how's it going?"

"Not bad, just trying to dodge the pariah every time I come and go from the hospital."

I groaned. "They haven't let up yet?"

"Nope. They're determined. You're the only thing they ask about. I've even been offered twenty thousand dollars if I spill. I guess they don't believe me when I say I have no fucking clue where you are."

"It should die down soon. I'm sorry you have to deal with it all until then. I'm intentionally staying away from the TV. People probably think I'm in a mental hospital by now."

She laughed. "Actually, that has been one of the rumors."

I scoffed. "Such bullshit. How's Nick doing?"

"Better, I think. The doctors are hopeful he'll wake up soon." That was good to hear. She sounded better as well. "What about you? Is dickface still being an ass?"

I chuckled. "As a matter of fact, no. I don't know what's up with him, but he's been decent today. You know that song I started writing a couple months ago?"

"Yeah."

"I think I found my muse. Maybe something good will come out of this tragedy after all."

"Wait . . . are you trying to tell me this guy is *hot*? How old is he?"

"Maybe five years older than me?"

"Send him my way then. Just do me a favor and don't fall for him."

I snorted. "Not gonna happen, trust me."

"Good. Remind me not to tell Nick about him when he wakes up. He'll be ready to fly out on a plane and get you. When this is all over, maybe you two can actually give it a shot instead of pretending."

"He knows how I feel about that. It would never work. We've already had a bunch of problems with the media and we aren't even really together."

"True, but I know he wants more. It would've been nice to have you a part of our family."

I smiled. "We're already family." Blake waltzed out of the building with something in his hand. "I have to go. I'll call you tomorrow."

"Okay. And remember . . . don't get attached. You'll be leaving there soon."

"You have nothing to worry about. I'll talk to you

later." I hung up and unlocked the doors just in time for Blake to reach the handle.

He opened the door and tossed something in my lap. "That's for you. It'll help your skin."

I read the label on the tube; it was prescription strength antihistamine cream. "Did you go in there just for this?"

"Don't get used to it, princess. I'm not a nice guy."

I smiled. "And I'm not a nice girl. Remember, you still have a payback coming your way."

He burst out laughing. "I look forward to it." He wouldn't be saying that once I got done with him.

As soon as we arrived at his ranch, we got out of the car and he grabbed my bag. "What made you change your mind about me?" I asked, following him to the door.

"Does it matter? I apologized for being a dick, didn't I?" He opened the door and held it wide for me.

"And I appreciate that." I held up the cream. "But the Blake I met wouldn't have given a rat's ass about my skin. I want to know what changed."

Sighing, he set my bag down. "Why do you care?"

"Because I do," I said, scratching my arm.

His gaze landed on my reddened skin. "I think we need to focus on one thing at a time." Taking the cream from my hand, he nodded toward the couch. "Sit down. I'll put this on your back."

Eyes wide, I gasped. "I'm not taking off my shirt."

He rolled his eyes. "You can *lift* it, not take it off. You won't be able to reach back there." Grasping my elbow, he gently pulled me to the couch. "Come on, I'm not going to molest you. I know your boyfriend wouldn't appreciate it."

"You mean Nick?" I asked, taking a seat on the couch.

He chuckled. "Yeah, I guess so. Not unless you have more than one. Nick's the hockey player right?"

Taking a deep breath, I lifted the back of my shirt, trying my best to keep my chest covered. "Yes, but he's not my boyfriend. He's my agent's brother. They thought it would get the stalker off my back if I made it known I was with someone."

"That worked well. Are you worried about him?"

I nodded. "More than anything. I hated having to leave him."

"He'll be all right. I've seen him play. He takes down everyone on the rink."

The thought made me smile. I missed watching him and the guys play. "That's what gives me hope. I just pray he'll be able to get back on the ice. Hockey is his life."

Taking the cream, he squirted some in his hands and rubbed them together. When he touched me, I sucked in a breath. "Is it cold?"

"No," I breathed. "It's fine."

"We should probably take you to get more clothes. Not unless you want to wash the same couple of outfits every day."

"Not really. But do you think it's safe to go out in public?"

You'll be fine. Plus, you have your new identity. No one in this town is going to believe Hadley Rivers is here."

I glanced at him over my shoulder and didn't realize he was so close. His fingers stopped on my skin, our lips were only a few inches apart. "Why is it so hard to believe? I like the mountains."

He lifted a brow. "Do you like hiking them too? I know they're pretty to gaze at, but there's so much you can't see by looking at them from afar. A city girl like you couldn't hang on the trails."

"Wanna bet?"

A mischievous gleam sparkled in his eyes. "How about this . . . we take you to get some new clothes tomorrow, then the next day, I take you hiking."

I loved proving people wrong, especially when they thought I couldn't do something. "What are we betting?"

He bit his lip. "Dinner every night for the rest of the time you're here. If you can't keep up with me on the trails, you cook. Sound fair?"

With a wide grin, I nodded and lifted my hand. I was planning on doing that anyway. "Deal. And if I win, you have to wear a pair of Mexican pointy boots for an evening out on the town."

He shook my hand. "I guess this would be part of my payback?"

"Some of it. But your boots need to be a pair that *I* pick out," I added.

"Oh hell," he laughed, letting my hand go. "That's not going to happen."

I turned back around, hiding my smile. He was going to lose. Taking a deep breath, I closed my eyes and waited for his fingers to touch me. When they did, I didn't want him to stop. They were warm and gentle as he spread the cream over my skin. Goosebumps fanned out across my body and a deep chuckle vibrated in his chest. My eyes shot open. Fuck, had I moaned out loud? Thankfully, he couldn't see my flaming cheeks.

"Are you about done?" I asked, feigning impatience.

"Almost," he replied. I could hear the smile in his tone. "Just a little more." As soon as he was done, he tapped my side. "You can lower your shirt now."

I dropped it and quickly moved to the edge of the couch. "Thanks."

"Want something to drink? After breaking out in hives and demolishing the waffle batter machine, I'd say you need one."

Groaning, I covered my face. "I will never forget that as long as I live. But a drink would be great. I don't care what kind." He tossed me the cream and I applied it to the rest of my body as he rummaged around the kitchen.

He came back into the room with an apple cider beer for each of us.

"Interesting," I said, taking one of the chilled bottles.

"Not exactly the champagne you're used to getting, but they're really good."

I threw a couch pillow at him and he dodged it, chuckling. "Whatever, jackass. I don't even drink champagne." We laughed together and it felt good to joke around. It made the whole situation more endurable.

He finished off his beer and lounged back on the couch, his gray gaze on mine.

"Who's the girl with you in that picture in your room?"

Jaw tense, he looked away. "Someone from my past."

"O-*kay* . . . care to elaborate?"

"Not really. But if you must know, she's the first and last girl I ever gave a damn about."

"Where is she now?"

"Out in California with someone else. We parted ways a long time ago."

"Do you miss her?"

"Not in the way you think. We've both moved on." His phone rang and he pulled it out of his pocket. "Robert, what's going on?"

Heart thundering, I sat up. Blake's expression hardened and I knew whatever he was hearing wasn't good.

"Are you fucking kidding me? That's ballsy. What the hell is he doing there?"

I heard Robert's voice on the other end, but I couldn't tell what he was saying. Blake hung up and blew out a frustrated breath. "What happened?" I asked.

He clenched his phone. "The surveillance cameras picked up an intruder at your house. When the police showed up, he fled."

Gasping, I threw a hand over my mouth. "Was he trying to come after me again?"

"I don't know, but if it's the same guy, at least we know he's not here. You're safe for now."

Yeah, but how long was that going to last?

CHAPTER 11

BLAKE

"What made you want to sing?" I asked, pulling into a parking spot in the middle of downtown. It was our first venture into Jackson Hole.

Hadley turned to me and smiled. "My mother. She sang to me every night before I went to bed. Granted, it was always Christmas songs, but she had the most beautiful voice."

It was amazing how gorgeous she looked with no makeup on, her blonde hair thrown in a messy ponytail. I wondered if anyone else ever had the privilege of seeing her like that. We hopped out of the car. "Why country though? I know a bunch of people give you shit because they think you're not the real deal."

Huffing, her smile faded. She joined me on the sidewalk, her arm brushing mine. Instead of playing the role of siblings, we decided it was best to be past lovers. "I don't see how anyone can say I shouldn't be singing country. My first song was about my mother and father, who in fact did grow up on farms in Idaho. He was her cowboy, her first and only love. They moved to New York before I was born. Once that song took off, the image kind of stuck. But then people found out where I was from. It's been a battle ever since."

"I know how that goes," I grumbled.

"How is that?"

"Once you meet my friends, you'll find out. First, let's find you some clothes."

Multiple outfits and an hour later, we were headed back to the car. "I didn't bore you, did I?" she asked, elbowing me in the side.

I chuckled. "No. It's nice to be around a woman who knows what she wants. That indecisive bullshit is what gets me." The shopping trip had actually been pleasant with her company, which was a first for me.

"I'm not like that, well except for when it comes to ice cream. There are just too many flavors to choose from."

I had to admit, she was different from the stars you saw on TV. "We can pick you up some when we go to the store. I need to make sure the house is stocked so you can cook me dinner when you lose the bet."

Hadley punched me in the arm. "You are so full of yourself. Have you always been like that?"

I winked at her. "It's part of my charm. The ladies love it."

"I bet," she said, rolling her eyes.

We were almost to the truck, but I took us on a quick detour. There was one more shop I wanted to take her to.

"You know, you haven't told me much about yourself."

I shrugged. "There's not really much to say. I've been doing undercover work for years. It's the only thing I'm good at."

"That's not true. You're good with horses. I've seen you with Snowflake."

"So you've been watching me?" I teased.

She smiled, her cheeks turning red. "Don't flatter yourself, jackass. But in all seriousness, you have a talent. You're gentle with them. Coming from your line of work, I never thought that'd be possible."

We reached the shop and I opened the door for her. "It took time. I've had help though. Tyla, the woman who works for me, is the best trainer in all of Wyoming. I wouldn't have been able to do it without her."

"Wow, that's cool," she said, genuinely impressed. She walked inside the store and I followed behind her.

"Where's she been? I haven't seen her around."

"She's out of town, but she should be back soon. Hopefully you'll get to meet her before you leave."

"Well, I'll be damned. What's up, city?" a voice called out.

Chuckling, I turned around and found a short, red-headed bastard with a scruffy beard grinning at me; it was one of my good friends, Mitch Bennett. We shook hands and I slapped his back. "What's up, cocksucker? It looks like it's a little slow today."

He shrugged. "It's off season still. It'll pick up at the end of the month. You know how it gets around here."

I snorted. "Tell me about it."

Tourists would come from all over the place to visit our national parks. There were also plenty of women who were interested in finding out what it was like to ride a stallion . . . and I wasn't referring to the horses. I'd learned the hard way to stay away from the tourists. I'd had one who didn't want to leave after I slept with her, and another one who wanted me to fuck her in the ass. I pissed that one off when I sent her packing out my front door. Needless to say, it was a learning experience.

Mitch smiled at Hadley. "I see our friend here is rude. I'm Mitch. Who might you be?"

She held out her hand and he took it, mesmerized. "I'm Anna. I'm visiting here for a few weeks."

"Anna, it's nice to meet you. Has anyone ever told

you how much you look like that country singer?" He closed his eyes, brows furrowed. "What's her name? Oh yeah, Hadley Rivers," he said, opening his eyes wide.

She shrugged. "I hear that from time to time, but I don't compare to her."

"On the contrary, you're much prettier. So what are you doing with this dumb ass? If you're looking for a true cowboy, I know where to find one," he said, waggling his brows.

I rolled my eyes while Hadley laughed. "She's visiting me from North Carolina," I informed him. "And she's not here to ride the short train."

Mitch grabbed his chest. "Ouch, that hurt. I can see when I'm not wanted."

Chuckling, I clapped him on the shoulder. "Actually, you are. I want you to show Anna around the shop. You're much better at explaining everything in here."

His eyes lit up. "It'll be my pleasure." He held his arm out to Hadley and she took it excitedly. "Let's go," he said.

They strolled through the store and I watched how her face glowed every time he showed her something new. Whether it was hand-carved furniture, or paintings on the wall, her enthusiasm had me astounded. Maybe she could fit in.

"Hey sexy," a voice murmured from behind. Her hands settled on my waist and I pushed them off.

"What the fuck do you want?" I growled. When I turned, Rayna stood there with a seductive grin. That shit wasn't going to work with me.

"I saw you walk in and I could've sworn you were with someone else. You haven't traded me in already, have you?"

"If I had, it'd be none of your business."

Her eyes narrowed. "You're not going to let the other night at the bar come between us are you? Trent and I are over."

"Like I give a shit. We had our fun and it's done, end of story. What don't you understand about that?"

Hadley noticed us from the other side of the store and walked over. "Is everything okay?" she asked.

"Everything's fine," I assured her.

Fuming, Rayna pointed an angry finger at Hadley. "Who the hell is that?"

"I'm his girlfriend," Hadley said, snaking her arm around my waist.

Rayna scoffed. "Blake has flings, not girlfriends. Stop thinking you're special."

Smirking, I put my arm around Hadley's shoulders. "Things change, especially when you find the right woman."

Rayna glared up at me and then to her. "Well, you can have him, honey. He's a dick anyway."

Hadley turned my face to hers and winked. "That

may be true, but he's one hell of a lover." She lifted up on her toes and nipped her teeth at me. I snaked my arms around her waist, pulling her in tight. I was about to kiss her but she jerked away when Rayna stormed out the door. "She's gone." She laughed.

Shaking his head, Mitch chortled watching Rayna marched down the street. "Damn, city, you sure do have a way with the women."

I shrugged. "I try. Unfortunately, it's not easy to get rid of them."

"Looks like Jackson Hole has a Don Juan on their hands," Hadley teased.

Mitch elbowed her in the side and then pointed to me. "Every woman in this city has tried to get a piece of him. It makes the local men jealous. But I guess a congrats is in order. I didn't know you were a couple."

"We're not." Hadley laughed harder. "I just said that to get Betty Rotten Crotch out of the store."

Mitch doubled over. "She probably does have a stanky-ass crotch. This one should know," he said, pointing at me.

Hadley's smile faded and she averted her gaze.

What the actual fuck? Mitch was going to pay for that. "All right, I think that's enough for one day." I put my arm around Hadley's waist. "You ready?"

She nodded. "Yep."

"Are you still going to hang out with the guys this

weekend?" Mitch asked.

"We'll see. I'm sure once Rayna makes her rounds, everyone will know about my new girlfriend. I guess we could always play along and make the rounds about town. What ya think about that?" I said, tickling Hadley's side.

She pinched my arm. "Don't think so."

We said goodbye to Mitch and once we were outside, she slapped me on the arm. "You're supposed to be hiding me away and protecting me, not parading me around town."

I tapped her on the chin. "It was a joke, Hadley. I'm not going to let anything happen to you. Besides, I'd rather not go. Every local in the bar will be trying to hit on you."

"Speaking of which, why does Mitch call you City? I thought you were from around here." We got in the truck and started on our way back to the ranch, but I wasn't in a hurry to explain the story to her. "Are you going to answer me?" she asked.

Sighing, I ran a hand through my hair. "He calls me that because I'm a city boy. I only moved here a little over a year ago from North Carolina, after my grandfather passed away. He left the ranch to me."

Smugly, she lifted her chin. "And you had the balls to call *me* a fake?"

"Oh, sweetheart, I most definitely have those." I

winked at her.

She pretended to look offended, but ended up laughing. I joined in when she had to wipe tears from her eyes. It was over the dumbest comment in the world, but it was the hardest I'd laughed in over a year.

CHAPTER 12

HADLEY

"Hey, princess, you ready to go?" Blake called.

I finished tying my shoes and grabbed the new jacket I had bought. It was early May, but had snowed that morning. Never in my life had I seen snow in May. I rushed downstairs and Blake was in the kitchen, packing our hiking gear. Instead of his usual ripped and worn jeans, he had on a pair of black track pants and a long-sleeved blue shirt. Also, the cowboy hat he never went without, sat on the counter, replaced by an old baseball cap.

"Wow, you look different today," I teased.

Grinning, he gazed over at me with those stormy gray eyes of his. "Is that a good or bad thing?"

I sat down at the bar and laughed. "It's a good thing, but the dirty cowboy look agrees with you. It's hard to imagine you as a city boy. Where in North Carolina are you from, anyway?"

He packed waters and snacks into his backpack and zipped it up. "Born and raised in Charlotte. My parents used to bring me out here to visit my grandfather every holiday and summer."

"Was he your mother's father or your dad's?"

"My dad's. He moved to North Carolina to attend Duke. That's where he met my mother. After that, he never came back, except to visit."

Glancing around the house, it had to be heaven growing up in the middle of nowhere, surrounded by snow-capped mountains. It was a dream come true. "I bet it would've been nice to grow up here. I'm from Lower Manhattan. My parents didn't exactly take me to places like this. All of our vacations were to beaches and resorts." Sighing, I gazed out the window. "Not that I'm complaining. I'm not. It's just . . . it's so peaceful out here."

His thigh brushed mine when he sat down beside me. I tried to hide my smile, especially when he made no effort to move.

"I guess you don't know what that's like, do you?"

I shook my head. "And I probably never will."

The room fell silent. I finally had some peace, but

it wasn't enjoyable. How could I when Scott was dead, Nick was fighting for his life, and my stalker was still out there hunting me? Blake bumped me with his shoulder. "You ready to go? We have a full day ahead of us."

Taking a deep breath, I slid out of my chair. "And when we get back, I'm going to order you some glittery pink Mexican boots for our next trip into town."

He shook his head. "Keep dreaming, princess. Remember, you lose when the first complaint comes out of your mouth."

I stalked past him to the door. "Then it's a good thing I don't plan on complaining. Let's go."

The entrance to Grand Teton National Forest wasn't far from Blake's ranch. We stopped at one of the visitor centers and I grabbed a few pamphlets on the various trails. One went over specifics of what you should do if you came upon a bear. The thought scared the shit out of me, but I kept quiet. The bet was, I wouldn't complain and I could keep up. I wasn't about to fail.

"There are so many trails. How are we going to pick one?" I said, gazing at the map in awe.

"I think you'd like Taggart Lake. It's surrounded by mountains and the water is as clear as glass. It was one of the first trails I did as a kid, except that was during the summer. We're probably going to be trekking through four and five feet of snow today."

I waved him off. "That's easy for me. We get plenty of snow up north."

"Okay, Ranger Rivers. Sounds like you got this under control. Let's get our trail on!" He tapped me on the ass and led me out of the center.

When we reached the trailhead, there were only three cars in the parking lot. "I guess it's a good thing it's off season. I bet this place is packed in the summer."

He snorted. "You have no idea. I stay away from all of these places during that time. Too many rude fucking tourists. It amazes me how some have absolutely no respect for nature."

We got out of the car and he hauled the backpack over his shoulders. "How much did you pack?" I asked, gawking at the heavy bag.

"You have to be prepared out here. These trails aren't exactly a walk in the park." Grinning wide, he strapped the bag to his back, and a holstered gun around his hips. "Let's see what you're made of, Hollywood."

I waved toward the trail. "After you, *city*."

Chuckling, he started off on the path and I had no problem keeping up. So far so good.

"Do you have a camera?" Everything was so beautiful, I hated not being able to capture it. Once I left, I was probably never going to see it again.

Blake stopped and opened a side zipper on the bag. "As a matter of fact, I do. Have at it."

He handed me the camera and I squealed. "Will you be able to email me the pictures? I want to remember this place. Plus, it's the perfect inspiration for my new song."

"I can do that, sure. But if we run out of time, you can just take the camera with you. I'll get it back somehow."

And just like that, I realized I'd never see him again once I left. Lifting the camera, I snapped pictures of the mountains, and a few of him. Before going home, I'd have to sneak pictures of him working out in his barn, wearing his cowboy hat and no shirt. I wanted to remember him.

"What are you writing about?" he asked.

We came upon a bridge overlooking a rapidly flowing stream; it sounded almost like a waterfall. I snapped a few pictures and smiled. "I just started it. Basically, it's about a guy and girl who fall in love. He's a cowboy who changes his bad boy ways."

His lips pulled back in a smirk. "You're not writing it about me are you?"

"*Please.*" I snorted. "I don't see you changing your ways. Besides, players don't fall in love. It would ruin their game."

He shrugged. "Maybe you're right. I'm not the kind of guy who can be tamed."

That was for damn sure.

The trail disappeared into the forest, hiding the sun with its blanket of treetops. I shivered as the temperature turned colder. "You never know, Blake. One day, you might find the right woman. She's out there somewhere."

"What about you?" he countered. "If Nick is just your friend, where does that leave you? You're not planning on keeping up the charade with him forever are you?" He glanced over his shoulder.

"No, but he's the only one who's been able to put up with the press. Before him, I was dating a guy I went to high school with and once my career took off, he couldn't handle it. My only solution was to date someone who knew the business. Then every guy I tried to date ended up being a douchebag. Thankfully, I met Nick and everything fell into place."

"Will you go back to him when you go home?" He climbed over a fallen tree and reached for my hand to help me over. When he didn't let go, I smiled and kept hold. The trail started to disappear under a blanket of snow and I figured that was why Blake held onto me. It didn't matter, I liked being close to him.

"Not in the way you think," I answered honestly. "When I go back home, I'm hoping that means the killer's been found. I won't need to pretend with Nick anymore after that." The thought of hurting Nick's feelings made me sick to my stomach, especially after everything he'd been through.

"Are you sure he's going to be okay letting you go?" he asked.

"He knows how I feel. We had a discussion about it right before he was shot. He's always tried to take things further, but I don't want to ruin the friendship we have. Plus, he's my agent's brother. If things didn't work out, it'd make things very awkward."

The lake was up ahead and I gasped when it came into view. It was perfect, almost as if it was a fake background. Blake pulled me up on a huge rock and let my hand go. "Not something you see every day, is it?"

"It's amazing," I breathed out in awe. I looked down at the water and it was so clear, I could see the details of the rocks below. We sat in silence and I took a gazillion pictures. When I turned the camera to Blake, he looked at it and gave me that smirk of his I loved. He had stubble on his cheeks, making it even sexier. "Will you take one with me?" I asked him.

"Why? So you can burn it when you get home?" he teased.

I rolled my eyes. "Oh whatever, it'll be something to remember you by."

Grabbing me by the hips, he pulled me onto his lap and took the camera. "You better not tell anyone I took a fucking selfie."

"Your secret is safe with me." I laughed. He held up the camera and I snuggled against him. After the picture clicked, I stayed on his lap and turned to face him. "Thank you."

We shared a brief moment, feeling something was changing between us. My heart pounded and I cleared my throat.

Blake handed me the camera. "No problem." I slid off his lap and he stood. "You ready to hike some more?" He took my hand, helping me off the rock.

I could tell he was waiting for me to complain. Instead, I held my head high. "Lead the way." Once we ventured away from the lake, the snow got really deep. I slipped a few times, but caught myself before falling face first into the snow.

Blake was a little ways ahead, but stopped and turned around. "You okay back there, princess?"

I waved him on. "Don't worry about me!" I shouted. Picking up my pace, I reached down and grabbed a handful of snow. Each step he took, I did double to catch up to him. My fingers were numb from the snow, but I was almost there. Just a few more steps . . .

Blake sidestepped and tackled me out of nowhere, making me scream. His feet slipped and we both fell to the ground, laughing as we rolled around in the snow. He ended up pinning me to the ground, his legs straddling my waist and his body flush with mine. I shivered and it wasn't because of the snow.

"You should know better than to sneak up on someone like me," he said. His eyes strayed to my lips.

"I didn't think you'd hear me," I whispered breathlessly.

"You'd be surprised what I notice, princess." He trailed a finger down my cheek to my rapidly beating heart. "Like how your heart is racing right now. I didn't know I had that effect on you." I blew out a nervous breath and he smiled, his lips getting closer to mine. "Tell me what you want," he murmured.

"I can't."

"Why?"

"Because once I say the words, I can't take them back."

He brought his hands to my face, his thumbs tracing my cheeks. "Maybe this will help." His lips closed over mine and I melted against him, willingly giving in. I'd never been kissed like that and I didn't want it to stop. I wanted more. He pushed his tongue inside and I moaned as the heat rose between my legs. Holy hell, I wanted him. Rocking my hips up into him, I dug my nails in his back and he growled, pulling away.

"Fuck, Hadley."

"What's wrong?" I asked, breathing hard.

He brushed the hair off my face and kissed me again.

"You make me want things I can't have."

I nodded. He said exactly what I was thinking. "I know how you feel."

CHAPTER 13

BLAKE

What the fuck am I doing? I'd wanted to kiss Hadley since the first time she'd opened her smart mouth, but being with someone like her would only cause me problems. Once she went back to California, she'd move on with her life and I'd only be a distant memory.

What did I care anyway? I could have a different girl every night if I wanted. The problem was, I didn't want just any girl. I wanted the one I could only have for a short while. That seemed to be a trend of mine, wanting the women who would never belong to me. *Reach for the stars*, my mother always told me. I literally was reaching for a star, a country star.

"Want some hot chocolate?" Hadley called out.

I threw on a shirt and joined her in the kitchen. She'd changed out of her wet clothes and into a pair of pink pajama pants and a tank top. She leaned over the counter, her tits bulging out of the top. Jesus help me, she was going to kill me and didn't even realize it.

"Actually, I'll just take a beer." I grabbed one out of the refrigerator and guzzled it down.

"Slow down there, killer," she teased. "You're not sulking because I won the bet are you?"

I threw the bottle away and pulled her into my arms. She came willingly and I could see she wanted me. It made my dick so fucking hard, especially when she rubbed up against it. She bit her lip and smiled, teasing me with her half-lidded blue eyes. What the hell was I going to do? I was supposed to keep her safe, not put my dick in her.

"No, I'm hoping if I get a buzz, those pink Mexican boots you order tonight won't look so bad."

She burst out laughing. "Speaking of which, can I use your laptop? I want to get those ordered up before you try to change my mind."

I nodded toward my computer. "Go. I don't want to spoil your fun. You just better not take any pictures of me in them. If I find them in a tabloid, I'll hunt you down."

Giggling, she pushed me away and grabbed my

laptop. "I think I might like that."

So would I. While she snickered at the computer, I started dinner. I wasn't about to trust a woman to use my grill. Stepping outside, I fired it up and watched the sun set behind the mountains. It made me wonder how many days I had to wait around while amateurs tried to find her stalker. She pounded on the window from inside. When I turned around, she pointed to my phone on the counter.

"You have a call," she shouted.

I rushed inside and scooped it up. "Yeah?" I answered, hoping I made it in time. I didn't have the number programmed in my phone, but I knew who it was.

"Mr. Evans, how are you?" he asked. It was George Rivers, Hadley's father. She was still searching for those fucking boots, so I snuck back outside.

"I'm fine. Yourself?"

"Can't complain. I'm calling to check on Hadley. Is she doing okay?"

I glanced back at her through the window. "She's fine. Have you not talked to her?"

"She doesn't exactly talk to me much these days. When she does, it usually ends in a fight. I just want to keep her safe."

"As do I."

"Maybe one day, she'll understand why I'm so

protective. If she only knew how many threats I got on her life every week."

"What?" I growled.

He sighed. "Only a few people know about this, so I'm trusting you to keep it to yourself. The last thing I want is for Hadley to find out. That's why I hired Scott to protect her. I had to know someone was with her at all times."

"Have any of the threats ever been carried out?"

"No. Most of them were just given to scare me, I think. It still doesn't change the fact they were threats. Does Hadley know I'm paying you?"

"No. I'll tell her when it's all over. I don't think that's something she needs to know."

He sighed. "Agreed. She'll see it as interfering. Just watch over my baby girl. She's all I have left."

"I will, Mr. Rivers. Hopefully, the case will be solved soon and she can go home." As much as I wanted them to catch the bastard, I also didn't want her to leave.

"I can only hope so. I bet it kills her not to be singing."

"I'm sure it does, but she's had time to write in peace. And having the privacy, away from constant cameras shoved in her face, is doing her some good as well. She needed a break."

"She *has* been pushing herself too hard." He blew out a heavy sigh. "Oh, before I go, I just wanted you to know I sent the money to your account, paid in full. It's a thank you for watching over my girl."

I swallowed hard. There was ten million fucking dollars in my account. "You're welcome, Mr. Rivers. We'll keep in touch." As I set the phone down, a feeling like I was deceiving Hadley hit my gut. But the things I could do to my ranch with that money would be phenomenal . . .

Would she understand? Probably not. She was a female with daddy issues.

"Everything okay?" Hadley asked.

"Yeah," I said, fumbling with the grill. "It was just a business call." I turned around and faced her.

She crossed her arms, rubbing her hands against her bare arms. With the sun gone, it was pretty cold. "I came out here to tell you I found the perfect boots. They'll be here in a couple of weeks. I don't know if I can take the anticipation."

"Thanks for coming out here to explain how you're ready for me to look like an ass." I chuckled.

She beamed. "You're welcome. Is the grill about ready? I'm starved."

"Almost. Come on, let's go inside." I grabbed my phone and put my arm around her. Her skin was freezing. Before we could get to the door, my phone rang again. "What the fuck?" I growled.

Hadley laughed and reached for the door handle. "You're Mr. Popular tonight."

"No shit." When I looked at the screen, my pulse spiked. "Robert," I announced, answering the phone. Hadley froze.

"How's it going?" he asked.

"Better. What's up?"

"We searched the grounds around Hadley's house and found a cigarette lighter by the back door. That's where the intruder entered the other day. Can you ask her if she has any friends who smoke?"

I put my phone on speaker. "Go ahead and ask her. She can hear you now."

"Hadley?" he called.

"I'm here," she said, moving closer.

"Do you have any friends who smoke? We found a cigarette lighter by your back door."

She chewed her lip, then shook her head. "Not that I know of. At least none of them do at my house."

"All right. We're going to check it for prints and see where that leads us. It'll take a few days but I'll call you with the results."

"Sounds good," I said and then hung up the phone.

"I hate thinking about that guy going through my stuff," Hadley said, shivering. "Do you think it's almost over?"

I shrugged. "Could be. We'll find out when they get the finger prints back. But that lighter could have just as likely fallen out of a friend's pocket months ago."

She nodded. "Hopefully this will be the break they need. I'm ready for the police to find this guy."

So was I, but as soon as they found him, she'd be flying back to California. As much as I wanted the case to be solved, I didn't want to let her go.

CHAPTER 14

HADLEY

The thought of going back home was both exciting and terrifying. I loved the solitude of being tucked away in cowboy paradise, but I wanted to get back to my life, to singing. My heart wanted both, but I knew it was out of my reach. And even more frustrating, Blake's heart was out of reach. Ever since Robert's call, he'd been acting distant. He kissed me before I went to bed, but that was it. I wanted more. Maybe I was too subtle? I don't know, but I planned on making my desires known.

Once I was dressed, I marched downstairs to tell him how I felt. I didn't exactly know what I was feeling, but it was something I couldn't ignore. When I approached the barn, I stopped dead in my tracks. *You have got to be kidding me.* Standing there, smiling at him from across Snowflake, was a beautiful, curly blonde, dressed in a pair of ripped jeans, a tight tank top, and boots. What the fuck?

Keeping my expression neutral, I strolled into the barn. Both of them turned to me and the woman smiled wide. "Hi," she greeted with a wave of her hand.

"Hey," I replied, turning my attention to Blake who was shirtless, glistening in sweat. He cleared his throat and nodded toward the woman.

"Anna, this is Tyla. She's the one I told you about. She works for me."

Tyla held out her hand. "It's nice to meet you, Anna. Blake told me you're from his old stomping grounds."

I shook her hand. "I am, but I have to say, he made the right choice moving out here. It's amazing."

"That it is. How long are you here for?"

My eyes met Blake's and he responded. "Probably not much longer. She has to get back to work. I can't keep her from it forever."

By the look on Tyla's face, she could sense the tension. "I see. Do you two want to meet up at the bar tonight? The whole crew is going."

Blake lifted a brow at me and I nodded. It could be fun. Maybe if he had a few drinks, it would loosen him up. "Sure. We'll meet you guys there," he said.

She turned and went back to Snowflake. "Good

deal. I'm going to take this wild one for a ride now. Do you want to join me?" she asked, smiling straight at me.

"Who *me*? On a *horse*?"

Tyla laughed. "Yeah, you. Have you never ridden before?"

I shook my head. The thought kind of scared me. They were so big and powerful.

Blake walked over to a stall and guided his black stallion out. "You can ride Nightshade. He'll be good to you." Nightshade blew out a puff of air through his nostrils and bumped me with his muzzle. Blake chuckled and patted him on the back. "He likes you."

Tyla hopped into Snowflake's saddle. "I'll be in the field when you're ready."

I glanced up at her and smiled. "Thanks." As soon as she left, I turned to Blake, eyes wide. "Oh my God, what if I fall off?"

Chuckling, he brushed the hair off my face. "Nightshade won't let you."

"Sure he won't. Famous last words." I shook my head.

He kissed my forehead. "You'll be fine. I promise."

"Hey, are we okay?" I needed to clear the air.

His brows furrowed. "Why wouldn't we be?"

I shrugged. "I don't know. After Robert's phone call last night, it was like everything changed. You seem a little distant."

"I know, I'm sorry about that. There's just a lot on my mind."

"Anything you want to talk about?"

He shook his head. "It's not important. Now come on, I'll help you up." Gripping my waist, he waited for me to put my foot in the stirrup before lifting me in the air.

Once I was secured in the saddle, and he'd placed the reins in my hands, my heart raced. It felt like I was a mile high off the ground. "Are you sure you don't want to come with us?"

"You'll be fine. Tyla's an expert rider. I'll be back here watching you. Just click your tongue when you want him to go, and use the reins to guide him in the direction you want to head. Pull back like this," he showed me the motion, "when you want to stop."

Taking a deep breath, I sat up straight and tightened my legs around the horse. I'd watched enough movies to hopefully have an idea of what I was doing. With a click of my tongue, Nightshade trotted out of the barn at a slow pace and headed straight for Tyla.

"Looking good," she said as we approached.

Gritting my teeth, I tightened my hands on the reins. "Thanks. Just as long as I don't fall off, I'll be fine."

"The only way you'll do that is if you let go." She glanced back at the barn before continuing. "So what's the story with you and Blake?"

"What do you mean?"

She laughed. "I mean, there's some serious tension between you two. I've known Blake for a while now and never have I seen him flustered over a girl."

"Really? Not even Rayna?"

Her eyes went wide. "Please don't tell me you met her?"

"I did. And I kind of told her we were dating. It was the first thing that came out of my mouth."

She giggled. "That girl is pathetic. Just a heads up though, she'll probably be at the bar tonight."

I shrugged. "No worries. I can handle her." Tyla started off toward the pasture and I kept up with her. "So you've never seen Blake serious about a girl?" I asked.

She shook her head. "Not since you showed up. I kept wondering when he was going to get his act together."

"What about you? From what I gather, he seems to be a ladies' man. How come you aren't interested?"

A smile spread across her face. "He might be easy on the eyes, but he's not my type. I prefer older men."

"Ah, I see. I guess that's my preference too," I laughed.

"Then why the tension? I was drowning in it back there. Have you two not . . ."

I huffed. "No, never. I thought I made it clear I

wanted to, but he hasn't followed through."

Tyla bit her lip, grinning mischievously. "What he needs is a little nudge. I'll make sure he gets that tonight."

"What are you going to do?"

"You'll see. By the end of the night, he'll be all yours. I know how the men around here work. The last thing they want is for another man to encroach on their territory. And believe me, by the way Blake was looking at you, you are his territory."

CHAPTER 15

HADLEY

I was never good at playing games. I might be shy, but when I wanted something, I wouldn't beat around the bush to get it. Why did Blake have to be so difficult? Once I was dressed, I glanced at myself in the mirror. My long, blonde hair was braided to the side and I had on a white sundress and cowgirl boots. It was strange because I didn't see the same Hadley in the reflection. I saw a girl who wanted a different life and different things. The only problem was that it wasn't possible.

"You will never be normal," I said to my reflection. "You never have been." Turning on my heel, I left my room and went straight to the kitchen. I held in my gasp the moment I spotted Blake. He sat at the bar, all cleaned up with a nice pair of jeans and a snug black T-shirt with his hair in messy spikes. No wonder all the ladies loved him; he was sex on a stick.

"I'm ready," I announced.

His gaze lifted, then darkened as he took me in. "Ho-ly fuck. You're going to get me kicked out tonight, princess."

"Why?"

"Because every guy in the bar is going to try to put their dick in you."

"Many have tried and all have failed. You have nothing to worry about. Are you ready to go?"

His eyes raked over my body again. "No, but it looks like I have to be. Just do me a favor and stay close." He started for the door and grabbed one of the light-weight jackets off of the coat rack, slipping it over my shoulders as we walked out the door. "It's supposed to be chilly tonight. Maybe you should keep this on."

"Are you sure you're not trying to cover me up?" I asked jokingly.

He chuckled. "Maybe."

We stopped at the truck and he opened my door. Instead of getting in, I faced him. "Maybe *you* should be covering up. You're the one all the women want around here."

"Does that bother you?"

"Should it?" I countered.

He shrugged. "I don't know. Maybe one day you'll let me know." An awkward silence fell upon us. I had the perfect time to tell him how I felt, but didn't take it. What the hell was wrong with me? It was the same problem I had with singing brand new songs; I couldn't do it in front of an audience. I had to wait and see what the people thought once they heard it on the radio. It would've been so much easier if he'd just tell me how *he* felt.

Once I was in the truck, he shut the door and got in. When we arrived at the bar, there were people everywhere. Almost immediately, I found Tyla's curly blonde head in the midst of a group of guys.

"There's Tyla," I called out. Taking my hand, Blake pulled us through the mass of people to get to her.

"What's up, Evans," one of the guys in the group shouted. "I see you got a new girl." I recognized Mitch but the other three I hadn't met.

Blake put his arm around me. "This is Anna, an old friend from back home. She's here for a visit. Anna," he said, pointing at the guys, "I'd like you to meet Liam, Michael, and Devon." Liam was the tallest with brown hair and brown eyes. Mitch looked like a midget compared to him. Michael and Devon both had similar muscular builds, but Michael had whitish blond hair and a kind smile, while Devon was more of the dark and mysterious kind with his black hair and brooding eyes.

I smiled. "It's nice to meet you."

"Want me to get you a drink?" Tyla whispered in my ear. "You look like you could use it."

"Yes," I pleaded. "Something with a little kick."

"You got it."

Blake pinched my ass when she walked off. "Need something with a little kick, huh?" He chuckled in my ear.

I wanted more than that, but I needed the alcohol to give me the courage to ask for it. I was such a chicken shit. The second Tyla handed me my drink, I guzzled it down. While the guys all talked, Tyla pulled me away and slipped me another drink; I tossed it back, my body feeling all warm and fuzzy. Blake glanced back at me and lifted his brows. I nodded to let him know I was all right.

"Sebastian should be here in a minute to ask you to dance. He said he would be here soon," she whispered in my ear. "And just so you know, when you're not looking, Blake's watching you. It's very . . . protective. Almost like a wolf watching his mate."

I snorted. "Now that's interesting. Watch a lot of the Discovery Channel?"

Her lips pulled back in a wolfish grin. "Something like that. But trust me, Blake's feelings are there. I can sense them. I've always been a good matchmaker."

We watched a bunch of people on the dance floor doing one of the many country line dances, but then the song changed and what came on next made me smile. It was one of my songs.

"Anna?"

I turned quickly. "Oh hey, Mitch." Blake came up behind him, eyes blazing.

"Wanna dance?" Mitch asked, nodding toward the dance floor.

"Actually," Blake held out his hand, "this is our song."

Tyla elbowed me discreetly in the side, pushing me toward him.

I took Blake's hand and smiled apologetically at Mitch. "Maybe next song?"

"Sure," he said.

Blake twirled me around and pulled me into his arms. "There won't be a next song. You're wasted."

"I am not. Two drinks are not going to get me drunk." The room did spin a little more than usual, but it was probably because he just swung me around.

"Whatever you say, princess." He laughed.

Smiling, I laid my head on his chest. It helped ground me. "I love it when you call me that."

"Princess?"

"Mm-hmm."

"It used to piss you off."

I lifted my head. "I know, but now you say it differently. Why is that?"

His gaze moved to my lips, but then he shook his head. "It doesn't matter."

"It matters to me. Are you ready for me to leave?"

"No. Why would you think that?" His thumb brushed along my cheek and I shivered. I loved it when he touched me. It was a craving that would probably never be satisfied.

"Then why are you being so distant? No matter how much you say it didn't, something changed after Robert's call. I want to know what happened. It's different between us."

"That's the thing . . . there is no *us*. It would never work out and you know it."

Those words felt like a punch to the gut. "So you're not even going to try? Would it make a difference to know I want this? That I want you. We could make it work."

He shook his head. "Even if that's what I wanted, we'd never see each other. You're not the only one with something to lose. Besides, tomorrow you're not going to remember saying any of this to me." The tears started to build and I didn't want him to see me cry. I tried to push past him, but he caught my arm. "Where are you going?"

"To the bathroom," I snapped, jerking my arm

away. I rushed away as fast as I could and disappeared behind closed doors.

Tyla barreled into the room. "What the hell happened?"

I flung my arms in the air. "He told me it would never work. He doesn't want to try."

She grabbed some paper towels and handed them to me. "He's being an ass. Lots of people have long distance relationships. You just have to put in the effort."

"I don't think he's willing to do that. Plus, he thinks I'm drunk and won't remember anything I'm saying."

Placing her hand on my shoulders, she squeezed and looked into my eyes. "Then you prove him wrong. Now dry your eyes and get back out there. Always keep your head high, no matter what anyone does to you."

I nodded. "I'll be out there in a minute." Once she left, I dried my eyes and looked in the mirror. *I can do this.* Taking a deep breath, I opened the door, determined to find Blake and try again. I wasn't going to give up.

A man stepped in my path and I ran into him. His hands came down on my shoulders, and I wriggled out of them in disgust when I smelled his liquor-reeking breath. He was tall and a little chubby in the midsection, with sandy brown hair and tattoos all up his arms.

"Hello, beautiful," he said with a crooked smile.

"Sorry, just in a hurry to get back to my friends."

"No worries. I thought I'd see if you were okay. I

noticed you got upset back there with that assfucker." He took a step forward and I had no choice but to step back. His hazel eyes stared at me as if I was prey; I didn't like it.

"Yeah, well, he pissed me off. If you'll excuse me, I'd like to find him so I can rip him a new one."

"Why don't I help you? I think it could be kind of fun." At first, I thought he was Tyla's friend, Sebastian, but there was no way she'd be involved with such a scumbag.

"No, thanks. I can handle my own battles." I tried to slide past him, but he side-stepped me. "So help me, if you don't let me by, I'll spray you with my pepper spray and kick you in the balls. Your choice." I was ready for a fight. Blake had pissed me off so much, I was floating on adrenaline and needed a way to release my anger. Unfortunately, I didn't have pepper spray. It was actually just hair spray. It'd burn like a bitch though.

He burst out laughing. "Feisty. I love it. You wanna show me how wild you can get? Just ten minutes with me and you'll never want to fuck anyone else."

I reached into my purse and grabbed the spray. "And ten minutes with me will make you unable to fuck anyone ever again." The second he took another step toward me, I jerked out my spray and let him have it. Shouting in pain, he covered his face, making the path from my foot to his crotch a clear shot. He fell to his knees when I kicked him squarely in the balls.

"You fucking cunt!" he growled, cupping his groin. He rolled back and forth on the ground, moaning in agony.

As I stepped over him, I said, "Maybe next time, you'll make the right decision."

Blake ran up to me, then saw the guy on the floor. "What the fuck is going on?"

The room started to spin. Blake grabbed my arm to steady me. "Dumbass over there wouldn't let me by. He went on and on about fucking me, and some other stupid shit. I told him if he didn't get out of my way, he'd pay the consequence. He didn't listen."

Eyes blazing, he pulled me out of the darkened corner and back to the bar where Tyla sat. When she saw us, she gasped and got to her feet. "What's going on?"

Blake pushed me into a seat. "Keep her out of the way."

"Damn, he's pissed," the guy beside Tyla said. He had sparkling blue eyes and whitish blond hair.

Tyla put a hand on his shoulder. "Anna, this is Sebastian. We were wondering where you ran off to."

Before I could reply, all hell broke loose. Blake disappeared to the back and came out, dragging the guy across the floor by his neck.

Wide-eyed, Tyla sat back down. "Oh shit. Did Trent

do something to you?"

"He said he wanted to fuck me and then I kicked him in the balls. I thought I handled it just fine." Everyone stood back and watched as Blake kicked the front door open and pushed Trent outside. "What is he going to do?" I asked, knowing very well what was about to happen.

Sebastian finished his drink and stood. "He's going to fuck him up. Around here, you don't mess with another man's girl." He started for the door, pushing his way through the crowd.

"Where are you going?" Tyla shouted.

"To keep Evans from killing that worthless bastard."

Everyone rushed outside, but I didn't know if I wanted to see. Blake's eyes had gotten so dark they almost looked inhuman. He was a dangerous man, a man who had killed people before. I was afraid to know what all he'd be capable of.

CHAPTER 16

BLAKE

Singleton wiped the blood from his lip and laughed. "How does it feel to know I touched your girl? Serves you right for messing with mine."

His hands on her was all I could fucking see in my mind. I poked my finger as hard as I could against his chest. "Touch her again and see what I do." Turning on my heel, I walked away. I'd dragged him outside to kick his ass, but he wasn't even worth it. I was about to walk inside the bar when he stopped me with his chuckle.

"That bitch would've loved it," he chided. "I can just imagine, lifting that little dress of hers and fucking her raw. I think I'll go for it next time, she doesn't know how good she could have it."

Everything inside me snapped. I wanted to be the bigger man and walk away, but I couldn't. Instead, I tackled him to the ground, pounding my fists into his face. Blood spurt out of his nose, but it wasn't enough. He needed to pay, to get it through his fucking head he was never going to touch her again.

"Evans, stop!" a voice yelled. Three pairs of hands pried me away. Tyla's friend, Sebastian, let me go. "What the fuck? Are you trying to kill him?"

"No, but he's going to wish I did." Mitch, Liam, and Michael all kept a hold of my arms while Singleton laid on the ground, whimpering. I backed away willingly, allowing Trent's friends to check on him.

"He's okay," Jacob shouted, helping Trent to his feet. He was one of Trent's friends and the same size as me, but he didn't dare intervene. It was because everyone knew Singleton was a fucking douche. Jacob helped Trent into the car and they sped away. As soon as they were gone, it was like nothing ever happened. Everyone went back into the bar, except my friends.

"At least you took it outside," Mitch laughed.

The other guys laughed too, but it was no joking matter. I hated guys like Singleton. He was lucky I didn't kill him. He needed to be taught a lesson.

Making my way inside, I barreled into the bathroom to wash up. Hadley didn't need to see me all messed up. I hissed as the soap burned my busted skin, but I scrubbed my hands clean anyway. Closing my eyes, I splashed the cold water onto my face and leaned against the sink. My adrenaline was too high. All I could hear was the pounding of my pulse in my ear; until the door opened that was, and then I heard her voice.

"Are you okay?" I didn't have to see her face to know she was pissed.

I glanced up at her reflection in the mirror, her arms were crossed, lips set in a firm line. "I'm fine. You ready to go?"

"Past ready." Turning on her heel, she tore the door open and stalked out.

When I followed her out, Tyla stood just outside and patted my arm apologetically. "Good luck."

I watched Hadley march to the front door. "Thanks. I'm gonna need it."

We walked in silence to the truck, but I knew the lashing was about to commence. And sure enough, as soon as we were on the road back, she started full force.

"Was kicking his ass *necessary*? I had already handled the situation."

"He was hoping you'd fuck him, Hadley. He targeted you on purpose."

"Who cares? I wouldn't let his dick get near my worst enemy. I was perfectly fine."

"How do you know?" I shouted, turning a serious glare her way. "What if he pushed you into the bathroom and raped you? Do you think you would've been fine then? He said he would try you again. I had to make sure he wouldn't."

She opened her mouth to speak, but then closed it. The rest of the ride home was silent, but it at least looked like she understood my reasoning, maybe. She was a female, so probably not, but I hoped for the best.

When we got back to the ranch, she went straight to the kitchen and pounded a glass of water. I sat down at the bar, but she had her back to me. "I didn't want him touching you, Hadley. I was walking away from the fight and I lost my temper. Just hearing his threat of coming after you again threw me over the edge."

Sighing, she placed the glass in the sink and slowly turned around. "I understand, Blake. I didn't realize he had done that. Have you two always hated each other?"

"It's complicated."

She snorted. "Let me guess, it involves a girl?"

"Yeah, but it's history."

"I see," she said, taking the seat across from me. Clasping her hands on the counter, she fiddled with her thumbs. "I'm not going to lie, seeing you so angry was a little frightening. It was like you were a different person."

"I think we all are when we get angry. Sometimes it can fuel our strength."

"Strong emotions can also lead to irrational

decisions," she added.

I looked into her bright blue eyes. "You're right, they can." Which was why I wanted to stay away from her. She wanted me, and I couldn't let her know how deep my wanting was for her. It'd be a mistake to let her in. Pushing my chair back, I stood. "I'm going to take a shower and get some sleep. You might want to drink a little more water. It'll help with the hangover in the morning."

She rolled her eyes. "I told you, I'm not drunk. I had a buzz earlier, but it's gone. I promise, I'm fine."

I didn't believe her for a second. "Goodnight, Hadley."

"Goodnight."

I wanted to kiss her so fucking bad, but I turned and marched out of the room. My dick was going to hate me once the mission was over. I'd walked away from Hadley several times and ended up with the worst case of blue balls. Why couldn't I shut everything off and just fuck her and not think about her anymore?

Once in my room, I kicked the door shut and went straight to the shower. A couple of my knuckles were split open but they didn't hurt anymore. It could've been the adrenaline talking. I took a long, hot shower until the aching feeling in my muscles surfaced. The room was full of steam and when I opened the door, it billowed out . . . that's when something on my bed caught my attention.

"What are you doing?" I growled.

Hadley bit her lip and dropped the robe she had on. *Fuck me.* I couldn't help but gaze down her body as she swayed up to me and pressed her tits against my chest. My dick responded instantly.

"I'm going to try this again, Blake. I want you, not just your body, but you. I've never felt this excited about anyone before. It has to mean something. You may say you don't want me, but I think that's a lie." She reached between us and wrapped her hand around my cock. I could explode right there on her stomach, but I held it back. Goddamn, this woman was going to kill me.

"Stop." Gritting my teeth, I grabbed her hand and pulled it away. I was either making the worst decision ever, or the best. It felt like the worst; especially when her eyes grew dark. "This isn't the kind of decision you want to make when you're drunk. I'm not going to lie, it's evident I want you, you're a beautiful woman, but being with me will only fuck you up. I can't do that to you."

Leaning up on her toes, she grasped my face and squeezed. "I'm not scared. Life is about risks. I want to take this risk with you."

I shook my head. "But I don't want to take it with you." It was a lie and I wished I could take it back the moment I said it. The level of hurt on her face would be something I'd always remember.

Grabbing the robe, she threw it on and ran out of my room, tears already welling in her eyes. I was a fucking idiot, but I refused to fuck her while she was intoxicated. Tomorrow would come soon enough and I could tell her how I felt. However, I had the feeling it was going to be too late.

CHAPTER 17

HADLEY
(Two Days Later)

For two days, I'd intentionally ignored Blake. Sneaking into his room was the single most embarrassing thing I'd ever done and I'd regretted it ever since. True, it might not have been the best decision at the time, but I didn't know what else to do.

Blake tried to talk to me on numerous occasions, but I pretended he wasn't there. I knew it was childish, yet I'd rather not face him than have to deal with the emotions. Anger was easier than rejection.

Tyla had just left for the day which sucked because I wanted to talk to her. Unfortunately, she was around dumbass all day. I couldn't talk to Felicity about it since she'd told me not to get attached. The last thing I wanted was to hear her bitch at me. On a brighter note, Nick seemed to be doing a lot better. I had that to lift my spirits.

A car door slammed and I rushed to the window. Blake had just gotten in his truck and started down the driveway. Breathing a sigh of relief, I rushed downstairs and found a note on the kitchen counter.

> **Gone to the store. When I come back, we're going to talk. You need to listen to me, even if I have to tie you up.**
> **~ Blake**

Tie me up? I wasn't going to give him the satisfaction. Hearing his voice was enough to drive me insane. It was like a shot through the heart each time he'd say my name. Talking to him was out of the question.

Taking a bottle of water, I guzzled it down and grabbed an apple. The weather was a little cool with the sun hiding behind the clouds, but it was perfect to be outside. Blake let Snowflake and the other horses out to pasture and it was always fun to watch them interact with each other. Snowflake always frolicked along like she was the only one out there, and Nightshade played it cool, hanging out by the stream. I climbed up on the fence and took a bite of my apple. Nightshade's ears perked up and he trotted over to me.

"I see how it is. You only want to come when I have treats." I laughed. He nudged me with his nose, his big round eyes trained on the apple. "Let me have one more bite and then you can have it." I leaned toward his ear and whispered, "Just don't tell Snowflake. She'll be angry."

Holding the apple on my palm, he opened his mouth and grabbed it with his teeth. "You're such a good horse. Why can't your owner be as sweet as you?"

The sound of crunching gravel caught my attention. I turned to the driveway. "Dammit! He's back already?" *Shit, shit, shit.* I patted Nightshade's nose and hopped off the fence. "I gotta go, boy. I'll give you another apple tomorrow." By the time I got to the barn and peeked around the corner, Blake had already parked his truck in front of the house. I was hoping like hell he didn't see me.

"Hadley, I know you're out there," he called. He took off his T-shirt and crammed it into his back pocket.

"Dammit," I hissed, crouching down low.

"Don't you think it's time we talked? You can't hide from me forever." His footsteps grew closer, so I hid inside one of the empty stalls, hoping he'd walk past. I slid down into the corner and held my breath as he walked by. "I want to say I'm sorry. I didn't mean to hurt your feelings the other night."

"Just drive the wedge in even harder, asshole," I mumbled to myself.

"I need you to come out and talk to me. I can make you if I have to, which might be kind of fun for me. You don't want me to enjoy this, do you?"

What I really wanted to do was smack him on the head. He was baiting me, but I couldn't figure out the game.

"Hadley?" His voice grew farther away until I heard his footsteps leave the barn. Once I heard the patio door of the house slam shut, I knew I only had a couple of minutes to get out of the barn. Taking a deep breath, I slowly got to my feet and glanced over the stall; the coast was clear. I had no clue where I was going to go, but anything was better than being stuck in a stall.

The wooden door of the stall creaked and I froze. *Fuck.* I held my breath and listened, but there were no footsteps approaching. As quietly as I could, I tiptoed my way to the back entrance of the barn and turned the corner, only to run right into Mr. Let's Talk. He reached for my hand, but I jerked away from him.

"You didn't think you fooled me back there, did you?"

"Fuck you," I spat, turning on my heel. I marched off but he followed close behind. "I have nothing to say to you."

"Well, too bad. I have a shit-ton to say to you. Now

stop being a childish brat and give me one minute."

Sucking in a breath, I froze. Did he really just call me a childish brat? Gritting my teeth, I faced him head on. I half expected him to smirk, but there was nothing but seriousness in his stormy gray gaze.

"All right, this ends now," I snapped, pushing on his chest. He stepped back, his jaw clenched tight. "You may think what I've done is childish, but I'm pissed and embarrassed. I show up naked in your room, just to have you turn me down; to tell me you wouldn't want to take a chance on me. I may have had a little buzz at the beginning of the night, but I was nowhere near drunk. It was the only thing that gave me the courage to tell you how I felt."

Huffing, I turned and marched out of the barn. "Now I just feel like a fucking idiot. So, by all means, make me sit down and hear all the reasons why you don't want to be with me. Go ahead and call me childish. I don't care anymore," I said, waving my arms in the air. "At least I wasn't afraid to let you in."

My heart thundered in my chest. It felt good to scream out my feelings, but now they were no longer mine. Anger could make a person say just about anything.

Out of nowhere, a rope lassoed around my body. I screamed when it bit into my skin, burning as Blake tightened it, roping me in. I struggled to break free, but it was so tight, even my hands started to tingle. I tried to stand my ground, but the harder he pulled, the tighter it got.

"Dammit, Blake. Let me go! I can't feel my hands." I had no choice but to willingly move my feet. If I didn't, he'd drag me across the ground through the dirt. My dignity was more important.

"You shouldn't have walked away," he growled, his voice by my ear. He jerked me around and pushed me into one of the empty stalls. I turned my face away, but he grabbed my chin. "I don't think so, princess. You're going to look at me when I say this. Do you want me to tie your hands and feet together too?"

I had no doubt he'd do it. "Fine," I spat, lifting my glare to his. "What do you want?"

His lips closed over mine, hard and raw as he forced his tongue inside. I tried to fight him off, but it was a half-assed attempt. Who was I kidding? I didn't want him to stop. Not to mention, I couldn't move. I was at his mercy, and I liked it. He pushed me into the wall, rubbing his arousal against me. Moaning, I bit his lip and he pulled away.

"You," he growled, leaning his forehead to mine. "I've always wanted you, even when you thought I didn't." He loosened the rope and pulled me into his arms, kissing me again.

My fingers tingled from the blood rushing to them,

but I was able to get his jeans unbuttoned. I didn't want to wait any longer. His cock jumped when I ran my hand down it, massaging him.

Blake grasped my lip between his teeth and groaned. "I'm sorry for what I said. It was lies, all of it. I never meant—"

"Shut up," I said. There would be time for words later. "Just shut up and help me out of this shirt."

His eyes sparked, then he lifted my shirt and unclasped my bra, freeing my aching breasts. I gasped when he closed his lips over my nipple, sucking it between his teeth. I grabbed onto his shoulders and everything inside of me tightened. I wrapped my legs around his waist and worked myself over his erection.

"Ah fuck," Blake moaned. He unlatched my legs and kept his gaze on mine as he unbuttoned my jeans and slid them to the ground. I stepped out of them and he slid his fingers between my legs. My eyes rolled into the back of my head as he pushed one inside, then another.

He pulled them out and stared at me when he put them in his mouth. The level of raw intensity in his gaze made me tremble. I'd never had anyone look at me like that before. Lifting me in his arms, I wrapped my legs around his waist and he walked us over to a pile of hay bales and gently laid me down. My breaths came out quick, my heart thumping in my chest. The anticipation was torture.

Blake brushed the hair away from my face, his arousal aligning with my opening. When he pushed himself inside, I cried out and dug my nails into his back, relishing the feel of him stretching me wide. His thrusts grew hard and fast. I was so close to the edge, I was about to explode.

He trailed his lips to my neck and bit down, his fingers digging in to my hips. "You feel so fucking good."

I rocked my hips against his and cried out as my release exploded through every nerve in my body. Blake followed closely behind, grunting as his cock pulsated inside me. My whole body trembled and I ached for more.

Still connected, he rested on his elbows and gazed down at me. "You okay, princess? At first, I thought maybe I hurt you."

I shook my head. "It was a good hurt. It's been a while since I've been with someone."

"Look, I'm sorry for everything I said the other day. I knew that if I had one taste of you, it wouldn't be enough. Letting you go won't be easy."

I grasped his face and kissed him. "You don't have to. I'm right here."

"But for how long?"

"As long as you want me to be." He didn't look convinced, but I didn't want to hash out the details while I was still enjoying the post-sex glow. "Hey, at least now I know what it's like to roll around in the hay. It'll be perfect for my song."

His lips spread wide. "Are you writing it about me?"

I shrugged. "Maybe. You'll just have to find out when you hear it on the radio."

"How are you going to write your music? You don't have your guitar."

He had a point. Mine was still at the house I never wanted to go back to. "I'll figure it out."

He winked and slowly pulled out of me. "I got you covered, princess," he said, getting to his feet. Slipping on his jeans, he handed me the T-shirt he had stuffed in his back pocket. "You might need this."

"Hello? Blake, you in there?" Tyla called out.

"Shit," he hissed. Grabbing my shirt and bra, he tossed them to me and rushed out of the stall. I quickly wiped off with his shirt and threw my clothes on while he distracted her. The rake was just outside the stall so I fetched it and pretended to work.

"Hey girl, what's up?" Tyla said. I turned and smiled at her, knowing my cheeks were bright red. Blake walked by and winked before disappearing out the other side of the barn.

I wiped my brow on the bottom of my T-shirt and realized it was on the wrong way. "Not much, just helping Blake clean these stalls," I said.

She snorted. "Uh-huh. I bet you were. You might want to tell that lie to someone who believes you. I can tell when a girl's been thoroughly fucked." She pointed at my clothes. "Your shirt's on wrong and you have hay all up in your hair. All I can say is, it's about damn time."

Laughing, I said, "Don't I know it."

"What are you doing?" Blake asked, taking a seat beside me. He glanced down at the papers in my lap and leaned over.

"Hey!" I shrieked, covering them with my hand. "No peeking. It's a new song. I can't let anyone see it until after it's done." After the day I'd had with Blake, and riding with Tyla, I had never felt more inspired to write.

"Will you sing it for me?"

Smiling, I folded up my lyrics and tucked them down the side of my chair. "Maybe. But I never sing new songs in front of people, except in the studio. I have this fear everyone will hate it."

His brows furrowed. "Why do you care? You're successful already. Your fans love you."

"It's not that simple," I said, turning to him. "When I write my songs, it's a part of me, a part of my soul. The thought of people hating them scares me. That's why I never sing newly written songs at my concerts."

"I can understand that, but I don't think you have anything to worry about." He kissed my cheek and got to his feet. "Wait here, I have something for you."

I wondered what it could be. The answer came when he walked out the back door. Eyes wide, I stood and gaped at the beauty in his hands. "Oh my God, it's amazing. Is it yours?"

He handed me the most beautiful guitar I'd ever seen in my life. It didn't even look used.

"I'm not musically inclined. Give me a gun and I'm good to go. It's actually my grandfather's. He fiddled around with it, thinking he'd have time to learn, but it never happened. I figured you could have it."

"*Have* it?" I gasped.

He shrugged. "Why not? I'm not going to use it. He'd be happy to know I gave it to someone who will."

I ran my hands down the shiny wood. It was better than the one I had at home. "Thank you, Blake. This means a lot."

Taking a seat in front of me, he nodded toward it. "Go ahead and try it out. I'd love to hear you play."

I'd never played one on one with anyone other than my mother. She used to love listening to me play. Taking a deep breath, I sat down on the edge of my seat and strummed my fingers across the chords. I hadn't realized how much I missed the sound. The entire time I played, Blake never took his eyes off of me. I wanted to sing for him, to let him hear his song, but I couldn't do it. It wasn't anywhere near ready yet.

"Do you think that's a good beat?" I asked.

"Is that the one to your new song?"

I nodded. "I think so. It's different from my other songs, but I think it'll work."

He leaned over and placed his hands on my thighs. "I don't exactly listen to country music, but I think it kicks ass."

"So you live out here, parading around in your cowboy getup, and you don't listen to country music?"

He shrugged. "What can I say? It's the look that gets the ladies, not the lame music."

"You're such an ass," I said, rolling my eyes.

"Hey," he said, his gaze serious. "I didn't say *your* stuff was lame. I like that you write your songs based on the people you care about. It's real. Your music has emotion to it."

"Thanks. I like to make people feel."

A small smile splayed across his lips. "You want to help me feel?"

Giggling, I set the guitar down and kissed him. "I think I might enjoy that. Where do you suggest I start?"

"Oh, I don't know . . . maybe in the shower?" His smile alone turned me on. He had those bedroom eyes that would be perfect for magazines.

Biting my lip, I grabbed his hands. "My shower or yours?"

He chuckled. "I don't know, I think we should give them both a go."

"Okay, but first I need to call Felicity. She expects me around noon, that way she knows to pick up the phone. Apparently, the media keeps harassing her for a story."

Blake shook his head. "Do you deal with that shit every day?"

"Not like that. There aren't too many people who have my phone number. It's going to be interesting when I get back though. My mailbox is probably full."

I wanted to talk to him about what we were going to do when I left, but I didn't want to ruin the moment. Everything was all new and vulnerable. The odds of the relationship working was stacked against us, but I had to believe we could make it work. Blake wasn't the type to balk at a challenge. Hopefully, he would see us as one and try to prove the world wrong.

When we got to his room, he disappeared into the bathroom and turned on the shower. I grabbed my phone and dialed Felicity's number. It rang and rang, but then she finally picked up and all I could hear were a bunch of people in the background, talking and laughing.

"Felicity, you there? It sounds like you're having a party. What's going on?" I said.

"That's because she is," someone else answered.

Gasping, I threw a hand over my mouth and sat on the bed. "Nick? Is it really you?"

He chuckled, then hissed in pain. "Yeah, it's me. Remind me not to laugh though. You'd think after two weeks of healing, I'd be up and moving around."

Blake leaned against the door frame, his body tense. When I looked at him, he stared back at me, but then averted his gaze and left the room. I wanted to go after him, but I couldn't.

"I miss you," Nick murmured in my ear.

"I miss you too. I hate that I couldn't be there for you. Everyone thought it best I left. As soon as they catch the guy, I'm coming home."

"What have you been doing all this time?" he asked.

All I could think about was Blake, but it wasn't the time to tell him about that. "Things you could never imagine me doing," I said. "But, I have to admit, I love where I'm at. When everything goes back to normal, I need to see about buying some property out here. It's been good for the creativity . . . and it's helped keep everything that's been going on off my mind."

He sighed. "I heard about Scott. Everything about that night happened so fast; I can't remember all of it. I'm sorry about what happened to him. He was a good guy."

My chest tightened. "It'll be strange going home and

not having him there."

"I know. You'll still have me though."

"And me," someone yelled in the background.

Nick chuckled again and cursed. "Stop making me laugh, fuckheads," he growled.

It was great hearing his voice. For the longest time, I thought I never would again. "Who are you talking to?"

"The guys are all here. Since the season's over, some of them are going back home. They wanted to tell me goodbye, but I think Kip and Dawson would rather talk to you than me. Kip's reaching for the phone, here he is." In the background, I heard a couple of the guys say they wanted to talk to me as well. I really missed bantering back and forth with them.

"What's up, sexy?" Kip quipped.

"Hey, Kip. How are you?"

"Good. But I should be asking how you are! The whole world thinks you've been locked away in a mental institution." I heard a smack and then I had to hold the phone away from my ear when he yelled. "Dude, what the fuck?"

Tristan argued with him in the background. "She doesn't need to know that shit. Give me the phone. You there, Hadley?"

"Yeah, I'm here. And it's okay, I already know what people are saying about me. I don't care. We all know I'm not suicidal."

"I know, but it sucks ass having to deal with that shit."

"I agree. So are you going back to Canada during off season? Nick said some of you were going home."

"Yep, that's why I'm here. It's a shame we couldn't have our annual throwdown."

"There's always next year," I said.

"Got that right. Well, I guess I'll hand you back to Nick. Be safe, wherever you're at. Hopefully you can come home soon."

"Thanks." The phone shuffled between hands.

"When do you think you'll be home?" Nick asked.

"I don't know. They found a cigarette lighter at the back door of the house. They're going to check it for prints. So far, I haven't heard anything."

"Keep us posted. Felicity left me her phone because she knew you would call. She went out to get me something to eat other than hospital food."

"Tell her I called, would ya? I should probably go." I could hear a heavy sigh, and then the line went silent. "Nick?"

"I'm here. I just don't want to get off the phone. Felicity said you hated the guy you were staying with. I can't help but worry about you."

I chuckled. "I'll be fine, I promise. He was only a dick at the beginning. It's not like that anymore."

"All right, I believe you. Just let him know I'll kick

his ass if he's mean to you."

I burst out laughing. "Pretty sure he would obliterate you. He's a trained killer, genius."

"Even so. The threat still stands."

"Okay, superman, get your rest. I'll talk to you tomorrow." I hung up the phone and bolted out of the bedroom. "Blake? *Blake!*"

I searched everywhere in the house and then headed out to the barn. When I saw Nightshade's stall empty, I knew where he'd gone. I walked out and took up my usual spot on the fence. The sun was going down, casting a warm glow over the pasture. There were no loud noises or car horns, and the smell of the air was clean and crisp. I was going to miss it.

"He loves me, he loves me not.

Oh, how I wish I knew. We haven't known each other long,

But when I'm with him, I feel like I belong.

He loves me, he loves me not.

My gray-eyed cowboy, I need to know.

Your heart may never be tamed, but I am not afraid.

Will you love me if I leave, will you love me if I stay.

Gray-eyed cowboy, please show me the way."

The words flowed through my mind so easily, I completely immersed myself in them. It wasn't until Nightshade whinnied in the distance that I was able to snap out of the haze.

Blake noticed me on the fence and guided Nightshade over, the hooves beating across the ground as they galloped to me. He had his hat so low over his eyes, I couldn't tell if he was angry. The closer he got, the more tension I felt.

"How's Nick?" he asked, voice clipped.

"He's fine. Why did you leave? I would've ridden with you."

He shrugged. "I needed time to think."

"About what? You're not mad that I talked to Nick are you? He's my friend, Blake. That's it."

His jaw tensed. "That's not why I'm pissed. I understand he's your friend and you were worried about him. And I'm also glad to hear he's awake, that's great news. But you need to know, I don't like to share. When you go back home, if you're planning on parading around in front of the press with him, I don't think I can do this. It wouldn't be good for me or you."

I nodded and lowered my head to hide my smile. He was jealous and I loved it. "Are you trying to say you want me to parade around with *you*?" I asked, meeting his gaze.

He huffed. "I don't know what the fuck I'm trying to say. What I *do* know is, if we're starting whatever it is between us, then we're going to do it right. I want the whole world to know you're mine."

And I wanted the whole world to know *he* was mine.

"Once all of this is over, you'll get your wish. But right now, you owe me a shower, or two."

He patted the saddle and reached for my hand. "Let's go then. I owe you a lot more than that."

CHAPTER 18

BLAKE
(Two Days Later)

I didn't like to consider myself the jealous type, but Nick was going to be a problem. Every time Hadley called, they stayed on the phone for an hour at a time. What made it worse was, she hadn't told him about us. The guy probably thought he still had a chance with her.

"Ready for dinner?" she called out, strolling into the kitchen.

"Yep. Which is why I already started it. I got tired of waiting on you."

She snorted. "I know what you mean. Nick could talk for hours if I let him."

I finished chopping the potatoes and tossed them in

the boiling water. "So when are you going to tell him about us? You're leading him on."

Sighing, she grabbed the lettuce and washed it off. "I'm not purposely leading him on. I just don't want to tell him over the phone. I feel guilty because he's in the hospital over me. Not to mention, my agent is adamant on me not getting involved with you."

"Why, because she wants you with her brother?" I snapped.

She shrugged. "Could be. But she also knows what happens to couples in our situation. The media will try to rip us apart."

"Only if we let them."

"Which is why we're going to be fine," she said, stuffing a strawberry into her mouth. "But I'm warning you, you have no clue what you're getting into."

I leaned over and kissed her lips. "I'm a big boy."

She giggled. "That you are."

My phone rang and since Hadley was closest, she snatched it up. "It's Robert," she said, handing it to me.

"What's going on, my man?" I answered. Putting him on speaker, I placed the phone on the counter and sat down. Hadley sat across from me.

"We identified the prints on the lighter. We're searching for the guy now. It looks like he skipped town a couple of weeks ago."

"Who is he?" I asked. Hadley perked up, chewing

her nails as she listened.

"His name is Dane Privette."

Hadley gasped. "Oh my God, I know a Dane. He works at the coffee shop I go to every morning. He's always so nice. Every day, he'd have my order ready when I walked in. Do you think that's him?"

"Yes, he works at the coffee shop off of fourth street. I'm sorry, Hadley. Sometimes you can never tell with people," Robert added. "And judging by the surveillance tapes, he fits the build and description. I don't know what he was doing at your house, but I'd have to say, it probably wasn't the first time he'd been there."

"Do you have any leads on where he went?" I asked.

"Yeah, his roommate said he was going to New York. We have people searching for him now. Don't worry, we're on his ass. He'll be found soon."

"Thanks, Robert," Hadley replied. "What happens when you get him? Do I go home?"

"Hell no," I cut in. "You're not going anywhere, until I look at the case. Trust me, the wrong people have been accused before."

"Which is why I'll send you the files," Robert offered. "I haven't forgotten the day you were arrested for attempted murder. I knew someone had to fuck up big time to bring you in."

Hadley gasped, but I shook my head. It was a long

story. "Call me when you find him."

"Will do."

I hung up and blew out a sigh. "Go ahead. I know you want to."

She opened her mouth to speak, but then closed it. "Have to say, it was a shock to hear you were arrested. But for murder?"

"*Attempted* murder. And believe me, it pissed me off when they brought me in. I was accused of shooting someone because the evidence had been planted in the trunk of my car. It's a good thing I had video surveillance around my house."

Her eyes went wide. "Wow, that's crazy. Who did it?"

That was the worst part. "Someone I used to work with. He deceived us all. Ever since then, I've learned to be very careful on who I trust. You need to be the same way as well."

"Does that mean I can trust *you*?" she asked.

As much as I wanted to say yes, I couldn't. "That's a decision you have to make for yourself."

CHAPTER 19

HADLEY

A waiting game; that's all it was. It'd been two weeks since they'd identified the owner of the lighter, yet they hadn't found him. He was supposedly near New York, which was good because that meant he was nowhere near me.

Now that Dane was the prime suspect and the police knew who they were looking for, Felicity wanted me back home. However, I wasn't ready to go back, not until they found him. Besides, Blake had been making sure to keep me busy . . .

"Your riding has gotten better," he noted. We were nearing the barn from an afternoon spent on horseback. Snowflake was almost ready to be given back to her owners, which made Blake sad. He tried not to show it but I knew he'd grown attached to her, and her to him.

Smiling, I scratched behind Nightshade's ear. "I've had a good teacher. I feel more comfortable than before. Maybe it's this big guy here who makes it fun." Nightshade snorted and I laughed. For the past two weeks, Blake had been showing me the proper way to ride. I didn't realize how fun it actually was.

"What do you want to do tonight?" he asked, sliding out of his saddle.

I climbed off of Nightshade and walked him into the barn. Before I could answer, a car came down the driveway. I pointed to the cloud of dirt. "Expecting someone?" When I got a good look at the vehicle, I burst out laughing. "Oh my God, I know what's coming."

Blake focused on the large truck and groaned. "Fuck, I was hoping they'd get lost in the mail."

Rubbing my hands together, I raced toward the driveway and he reluctantly followed. "I know what we're doing tonight," I announced excitedly.

When the driver got out, he waved at Blake. His nametag said he was Grady. "How's the horse training going, son?"

Blake waved back. "Pretty good. It's hard to let 'em go once you've got 'em all nice and trained in."

"I hear ya, I hear ya. Say, got a large package for you today." He slipped into the back of the truck and brought out a large, rectangular box. I slapped a hand over my mouth to keep from laughing.

"How big are those fucking things?" Blake growled in my ear.

I snickered. "I just hope you can walk in them."

"Here you go," Grady said, passing the box to him.

Plastering on a fake smile, Blake nodded at him and then grimaced at me. "One hour downtown, that's it." He tried to walk past me, but I stepped in his way.

"That's not our deal. But if you want to cut it down, you have to do something else in return."

"What?" He sighed in defeat.

He wasn't about to get away with just an hour of wearing those boots. Not after he'd made my life hell. "You have to go into one of the bars and dance to a song, that's it."

"By myself?"

I nodded. "Yep. I want to see if you know how to have some fun."

His lips tilted up in a smirk. "I think you know the answer to that. You've been with me for a month now."

It was strange to think I'd been gone that long. The past two weeks of it had flown by. "We have lots of fun together and I love it, but I want to see you dance. You owe me, after being such a dick."

He ran a hand through his hair. "Fuck, I'm going to look like a goddamn moron. I hope you enjoy this."

Giggling, I skipped to the door and held it open for him. "Oh, I will, and I'll have your camera nice and ready for it too."

He carried the box inside and disappeared to his room, cursing the entire way.

It was going to be a memorable night.

"This is fucked up," Blake grumbled as we got out of the car. There were a couple of girls who walked by pointing and laughing; it was epic. His boots were so long he couldn't even drive. It was the first time I'd driven in a month.

Taking out the camera, I snapped a photo of him just as another woman walked behind him trying to hide her smile. "Get to steppin'," I told him. "The sooner you start, the sooner the hour will be over."

"You're walking with me, aren't you?"

Laughing, I shook my head. "Nope. This is all you. I'll be a safe twenty feet away. I don't want anyone knowing I'm with you."

He brushed off his shoulders and started walking. "All right. Just don't get pissed when I score a couple of dates."

"Do that and I'll cook you dog food for dinner."

I had no doubt he could attract the ladies, even

looking as ridiculous as he did in his red and black plaid shirt, tight jeans, and bright red Mexican pointy boots. All the ladies would have to do is look at those gray eyes of his underneath the rim of that cowboy hat and they'd melt.

Over the next hour, I took picture after picture of people hiding their laughs. There were even some who wanted their picture taken with him; most of them looked like tourists. His picture would probably end up in their vacation photo albums, a keepsake of their time in Wyoming. I had about a dozen photo albums already with all the pictures I took.

"I think your camera's full," I called out.

He glanced at me over his shoulder and turned around with a smug smile on his face. "Does that mean you're done watching me with all the ladies? I saw you getting jealous back there."

I rolled my eyes. "Whatever, Evans. I'm not the jealous type." It was a complete lie, but I wasn't going to tell him that. There were several women whose hands slid a little lower than his waist when they were getting their picture taken with him. I bit my tongue and let it slide, even if I did want to break their hands. "You still have one task left, then we can go home."

Groaning, he took his hat off and ran a hand through his hair. "Fine, let's get this shit done."

He took off toward the bar and I laughed the entire

time. When we walked inside, there weren't too many people in there, but the whole place fell silent as he stopped in the middle of the dance floor. There was an old juke box in the corner and I wasn't surprised to see the song I wanted on the list . . . *Cotton Eye Joe.*

"Dude, what the fuck ya doing?" someone shouted with a laugh.

Giggling, I slipped in the money and pressed the button. The second the song came on, Blake sighed and then moved across the dance floor, kicking his feet up and holding onto the huge belt buckle at his waist — true Cotton Eye Joe style. The crowd cheered and clapped for him and so did I. I was able to get a few more pictures of him before the camera died. Those were definitely going home with me.

I felt a tap on my shoulder and turned around. It was Blake's friend, Liam. "Did he lose a bet or something?" he asked, chuckling as he watched Blake on the dance floor.

I laughed. "Yep. Just make sure to give him grief about it every time you see him."

"Hell yeah. I can promise you that."

I looked down at his green scrubs. "You're a doctor?"

He finished his beer and nodded. "Going on ten years now. Is it hard to believe a guy like me could be one?"

I held up my hands. "No, not at all. I guess I just

figured you'd be in the ranching business, like Blake."

He burst out laughing. "Someone has to take care of these idiot cowboys when they get hurt. Evans was one of my most frequent patients when he first moved out here. Those horses loved to buck him off."

Blake finished dancing and headed straight over. "Telling lies about me, doc?"

Liam shook his hand. "Nope, just enjoying the show. Thanks for the entertainment. Now I need to get home to the wife before she starts to wonder where I'm at."

Blake put his arm around me. "I hear ya. I need to get this one home to dole out a little payback for making me look like a fucking idiot."

Liam snorted. "You do that all on your own, so don't pass blame onto her." Blake slapped him on the back and they both laughed. "Have a good night you two," Liam said before strolling away.

I moved out from under Blake's arm. "Payback, huh? You lost the bet, fair and square. I don't think I deserve retaliation of any kind."

He leaned closer and whispered in my ear. "Not *that* kind of payback, princess. I'm pretty sure you'll like what I have in mind."

The second we got inside the house, he lifted me in his arms and carried me into his room. For the past couple of weeks, it had been my room as well. I felt safe with him, and worst of all, I was falling in love with him. It was dangerous to want a man like Blake, but I couldn't resist him. Setting me down, he unzipped the back of my dress and let it fall to the floor. I slid my underwear off and crawled back on the bed while I watched him unbutton his shirt, one button at a time.

"You love to keep me waiting, don't you?"

He winked. "Someone has to. You can't always have what you want, when you want it."

I narrowed my gaze. "Wanna bet?"

Grabbing his waistband, I playfully nibbled on his jean-covered arousal as I unzipped and lowered his pants and boxers. He sucked in a sharp breath when I wrapped my lips around his tip and flicked it with my tongue.

He fisted his hands in my hair. "Damn, baby."

I sucked him off as hard as I could, his moans making me wet between my legs. I wanted him inside me. "Lie down," I whispered. Sliding back on the bed, I patted the space beside me.

Smirking, he spread my legs instead and rubbed his cock against my clit. "I know what you're up to, princess. It's not going to work."

I bit my lip and smiled. "Then come here and give it a try. Let's see how long your control lasts."

Blake loved to be in control and it showed in the way he made love to me. Sometimes, it felt good to challenge him and take the lead. His raw gaze penetrated down to my core as he lay back on the bed, taunting me by licking his lips.

Straddling his waist, I leaned down to kiss him, sliding my clit up and down against the length of his cock. He dug his fingers into my hips and groaned as I rolled my hips over him.

"If you don't fuck me now, I'm going to take you myself, princess."

I giggled. "Don't like being teased?"

He bit my lip and sucked. "Not when I want you this bad," he said, voice raw and dark.

Core tightening, I lowered onto him and sat all the way down. He hissed and grabbed onto my hips, thrusting up into me. I rode him hard and then even harder when he sat up, pulling me into his lap. His mouth found my nipples, sucking and biting, as I milked him.

"I'm so close," I cried, holding him tight. Everything exploded all around me and I screamed out my release. He pushed me down onto him, his cock pulsating as he filled me with his warmth. His body jerked and he moaned. Breathing hard, I sat there on his lap while I caught my breath.

"I didn't think it was possible, but you made me lose control," he murmured.

Grinning from ear to ear, I leaned back. "You liked it though, didn't you?"

He shook his head and then kissed me, his body still connected to mine. "No . . . I fucking loved it."

CHAPTER 20

BLAKE

"What do you want to watch?" Hadley yelled from across the room. She flipped through the channels, going ninety miles an hour.

How the hell could she see what was on? I grabbed a beer from the refrigerator and joined her on the couch. "If football was on, I'd say we could watch that. The Carolina Cougars have been killing it."

She handed me the remote. "That's because Cooper Davis has been kicking ass at quarterback."

I coughed and almost choked on my beer. "You watch football?"

"Yeah, all the time. Cooper is one of my favorites. I met him when I sang at the last Super Bowl."

"Would I be name dropping if I said I personally knew him?"

Her eyes went wide. "No way, really?"

"Yep. There was a bar in downtown Charlotte where we used to hang out all the time. Sometimes I miss being back there." Hadley snuggled into my side and I put my arm around her. She'd been with me for over a month and I knew it was only a matter of time before she had to leave.

"When was the last time you went back?" she asked.

"Over a year now. I don't have any siblings and both my parents like to travel, so it's not like I have anything to go back to."

"That must be fun to travel the world. One day I hope to be able to do that when I'm not stuck on a tour bus. Are they retired?" She turned to look up at me.

I nodded. "For two years now. They decided it was time to live life to the fullest. You never know when your gig is up."

She blew out a heavy sigh. "My parents were like that, but my mom didn't have much time. It's not fun watching someone you love suffer."

I swallowed hard and rubbed her shoulder. "I know. I've been through that as well."

"What?" she gasped, eyes wide in surprise. "Who?"

"My mother," I said. "She was diagnosed with breast cancer and was lucky to survive. I didn't want to tell you because I knew it would bring up bad memories and only make you upset."

She held up a hand, trying to hold back tears. "I'm glad you told me. Every once in a while, I'll donate all of the proceeds of one of my concerts to charities who help take care of cancer victims. My goal is to help others before it's too late. I've seen the look on a child's face that just lost a parent to cancer. It breaks my heart."

"That was one of the things I found out about you that made me realize you weren't just a spoiled bitch who only thought of herself," he mumbled.

She smiled. "Gee, thanks. On a brighter note though, I want you to introduce me to the Carolina Cougars. I need to meet some famous people," she said with a wink.

"I doubt you have issues with that. Besides, I don't know if I want you to meet them. You might want one of them over me. They're famous."

She smacked me on the thigh. "Just because you're famous doesn't make you a good person. I like you for who you are. I don't need someone who's famous or rich to be by my side."

"Then what do you need?"

Her gaze met mine and she smiled. "You."

I leaned over and kissed her lips, burying her into the couch. She spread her legs and wrapped them around my waist. "Are you sure I'll be enough?" I asked, pushing into her.

She snickered and rocked her hips. "Definitely."

I went to pull her shorts down, but the remote was under her and the TV volume grew steadily louder. "Hold on," I said, searching for it underneath her body. Finding it, I was about to turn the TV off, when I looked at the screen.

"What is it?" Hadley asked.

Her head turned to the TV and she froze the second her name came over the news. *"Apparently, the driver is the suspect they've been looking for in the shooting at Hadley Rivers' home, where her bodyguard and boyfriend were both shot. There has been no word on where Hadley is at the moment, but it is believed she's in protective custody as the police have been searching for the suspect. We'll continue to show you live coverage as the pursuit unfolds."*

"Holy shit." I grabbed Hadley's hand and helped her up.

She cupped a hand over her mouth. "What the hell is Dane doing? There's no way he can escape from that many police cars."

"He must be desperate." A sickening feeling sank in my gut. High speed chases rarely ended well. I grabbed my phone off the coffee table and dialed Robert's number.

"Evans," he answered.

"What's going on?" I barked.

Robert blew out a frustrated sigh. "We found the crack house where Dane's been staying. When the NYPD busted in, he jumped out the window and drove away. He's clearly high as a fucking kite. If he hurts anyone during this pursuit, I'm going to kill him."

"Jesus Christ. Call me when you know more." I hung up and filled Hadley in.

"How long do you think this will go on?" she asked.

I shook my head. "Don't know. I just hope he doesn't kill anyone."

The pursuit lasted for another thirty minutes and ended with Dane running his car head first into a semi-truck. I knew without a doubt the fucker was dead. My phone rang but I kept my eyes on the TV when I answered. I already knew who it was going to be. "Robert."

"I'm assuming you know why I'm calling?"

I closed my eyes. "He's dead."

"Yes. Good news is, once we get everything handled, it'll be time for Hadley to go home. I know that'll make you happy. I'll call her father and get her out of your hair. He'll be ecstatic to see her."

"Nah, that's not necessary. I'll do it. Just give me a couple of days." I set my phone down and looked at Hadley. "Dane's dead. You'll be able to go home soon."

She shook her head. "I'm not going anywhere. The last thing I want is to deal with the press when all of this is going down. I just need a couple of weeks."

"You know your agent isn't going to like this. Everyone's going to want you back."

"I don't care. If you want me to go, I will, but I'm not ready to leave yet. I need a little more time. Everyone will just have to understand."

I pulled her into my arms and breathed a sigh of relief. I wasn't ready for her to go either.

CHAPTER 21

BLAKE

"You're going home today, girl." I rubbed Snowflake's muzzle. She huffed and bumped me with her nose. She wasn't the only one I was losing. Hadley's two weeks were up and first thing in the morning, she'd be on her way back to California. I didn't think it'd be so hard to let her go.

Grabbing the brush, I slid it down Snowflake's body so her coat would shine. It was a special day for Josie and I wanted it all to be perfect for her.

My phone rang and when I set down the brush, Snowflake snorted. She loved it when I brushed her. "Give me one second," I told her. I looked at the phone and smiled. "Well, I'll be damned," I said, answering the phone.

"Have you missed me?" Mason joked. Mason Bradley was the leader of our undercover group and an MMA legend. Not only was he a heavyweight UFC Champion, but he had solved one of the most heinous crimes in the sport.

Chuckling, I leaned against the wall. "You're damn right, I have. What ya been up to?"

"Nothing much, just taking a break. I heard you were watching the Rivers girl. That must be a pain in the ass. Don't people know you're not a bodyguard?"

"I don't think they got that memo. Besides, it hasn't been too bad; she leaves tomorrow. What can I do for you?" I asked.

"I have a job for you. Well, for me and you. It looks like I called at the right time."

"What's going on?"

"There's a situation out in Texas, where a couple of girls were found dead in a barn. The owner of the property is an elderly man in his nineties. I think his ranch hand is the one who did it, but no one can find him. I could really use your knowledge on this one."

I glanced at the house where my bedroom light glowed through the blinds; Hadley was awake. "When do you need me?"

"Tomorrow, if at all possible. I'll send you the details."

"Sounds good, brother. I'll be ready." Sighing, I hung up the phone and dialed Robert's number.

"Hello," he grumbled.

"I'm going to need you to escort Hadley home. Can you fly out here by tomorrow morning?"

He yawned. "Why can't you do it?"

"Mason just called and asked if I'd help him with a job in Texas. I leave tomorrow."

"All right, I'll be there first thing." We hung up and I got back to brushing Snowflake. I only had one more night with Hadley before we parted ways. Now all I had to do was tell her I wouldn't be going with her.

CHAPTER 22

HADLEY

"Aren't you ready to come home?" Nick asked.

I wanted to get back to singing, but I didn't want to leave Blake. "I am," I lied, hoping he couldn't hear the trepidation in my voice.

"I've been given permission to get back on the ice in limited practice. The wound still hurts, but I should be able to play again soon. Everything will go back to normal."

No, it wouldn't, but I couldn't tell him that yet. I wanted to wait until we were in person. He sounded so happy over the phone. "That's great, Nick. I know how excited you are about playing again. I think when I get back, I'm going to find somewhere else to live. I just can't bring myself to stay in that house."

He sighed. "I understand, baby. I'm sure the team will be happy to help you move."

I watched Blake through the window, talking to Snowflake's owners. He was handing her over to them. "Thanks, Nick. I think I need a new start."

"And I'll be with you every step of the way. But here's Felicity. She's been dying to talk to you. I miss you and I can't wait to see you again."

"Same to you."

"Bye, babe. I'll see you at the airport."

"Okay."

He handed the phone to Felicity. "Can you believe our lives are about to go back to normal? Do you have any idea how many people have missed you?"

"A lot?" I laughed.

"You're damn right. And you have a few concerts to make up too. I hope you'll be ready by next weekend?" she asked excitedly.

"I'll be ready, don't worry. Where am I going first?"

"New York, baby! I know you're excited about that."

I was, but my heart wasn't. Leaving was going to be harder than I thought. "You know it."

"All right, I'm going to get off so I can get back to work. We're going to have a welcome home party for you when you arrive. It'll be so much fun."

I said goodbye to both of them and made my way

outside. Blake was cleaning out Snowflake's stall. Without saying a word, I went up behind him and put my arms around his waist. He was sweaty, but I didn't care. "You okay?"

He chuckled and set the rake down before closing his hands over mine. "Did you think I was going to cry?"

"Not really, but I know I would if I was that close to Snowflake. I know you've grown attached to her."

"I have, but it's not like I won't see her again. The Wright's live just down the road. I'm sure Josie will bring her by to visit." He pulled me around to face him.

We stared at each other and all I wanted to do was tell him not to let me go. Too bad I didn't have a choice. I had to go. Lifting up on my toes, I wrapped my arms around his neck. "What's on the agenda for my last night here?"

His gaze darkened, but then he smiled and kissed me. "I have it all planned out. I just have to finish up out here and then take a shower. Why don't you grab a glass of wine in the meantime?" He slid his hand up my sundress and smacked my butt.

"Hey," I said, stepping away from him. "What are you up to?"

He winked. "It's a surprise. Now go."

I went inside and poured a glass of wine while he finished up in the barn. Tyla showed up and handed him something, but I couldn't see what it was. I wanted to tell her goodbye, but she left before I could catch her.

"Give me ten minutes and I'll be ready to go," Blake said as he shot past me to the bedroom. Once the ten minutes were up, he joined me in the kitchen, dressed in a pair of jeans and a white T-shirt. "Let's go." Taking my hand, he led me out to his truck and opened the door.

"Where are we going?"

He flashed a small smile. "You'll see." Shutting the door and jumping in his side, he started up the truck. Instead of going down the driveway, he pulled us around to the backyard and into the pasture.

"You're not kidnapping me, are you?" I joked.

He chuckled. "If I could get away with it, I would. It's going to be quiet around here without you."

"I know the feeling. Luckily, I have a lot to do when I get home. Felicity already has me booked in New York next weekend. It feels like it's been forever since I've been on stage."

"How's the new song coming along? Have you finished it?"

"Almost. I still need a good ending. Hopefully, it'll come to me soon."

He reached for my hand and squeezed. "You'll figure it out. I wish you would sing it to me. It's not the same listening to you in the shower."

I gasped. "You've been spying on me?" I smacked him on the arm and he burst out laughing.

"Hey, it's the only time I could catch you singing."

"You're such a creeper," I teased.

He shrugged. "You need to get over your fear, Hadley."

I wasn't afraid to sing in front of thousands of people I didn't know, but if I sang in front of him, it'd make me vulnerable. He'd see right through me. I wasn't ready for him to see me like that. The truck began to slow and we came to a complete stop.

"All right, we're here," he said, getting out of the truck. We were in the middle of nowhere, with wide open fields all around us. There were a few bison off in the distance and I prayed they stayed far away.

I got out of the truck and watched him climb into the back. There was a basket and a cooler, along with another box I couldn't see inside of. "What are we doing all the way out here?"

Smiling, Blake pulled out a bunch of blankets from inside the box and spread them out in the bed of the truck. "I thought we could have dinner and spend the evening out here, alone." Extending his hand, he helped me into the back of the truck and I sat down on the smooth, fluffy blankets. He opened the basket and pulled out various containers of food.

"Is that what Tyla brought this afternoon? I saw her hand something to you and leave."

He chuckled. "She's a really good cook, so I called in a favor."

"I wish I could've said goodbye. Will you tell her for me?"

"She'll be by in the morning. You can tell her yourself."

The food smelled amazing, and I piled a bunch of it onto my plate. She'd made roasted chicken, asparagus, mashed potatoes, and rolls. It all tasted like heaven. "Remind me to tell her how amazing this was before we leave," I noted. Blake averted his gaze to his plate, his body tense. "Is everything okay?"

"I got a phone call this morning, about my next mission."

When he looked at me, my heart sank. "Okay, so what does all of this mean?"

Sighing, he set his plate down. "It means, I won't be able to take you home tomorrow. Robert is going to fly over and escort you back."

My eyes burned and my chest ached. I knew we were going to have to say goodbye, but I was hoping I could coerce him to stay a few days in California. I wasn't ready to let him go. "I see. What kind of mission are we talking about? Is it dangerous?"

"Everything I do is dangerous, princess," he murmured.

Nodding, I focused on my plate. I didn't want him to go on another mission. Was that how it was going to be for the rest of his life? "How long will you be gone?"

"I don't know. It all depends on what happens. But as soon as it's over, I'll come see you, wherever you are."

Swallowing hard, I nodded again and quickly wiped under my eyes.

Blake moved over and put his arm around my shoulders. "Baby, don't cry. You know our lives are completely different. You'll be leaving me to sing at your concerts and I'll be leaving to go on my missions. I don't know what else to do."

"I know. I guess I just thought things would be easier. I have one night left with you and then everything's going to change. I'm afraid I'll never see you again."

Holding me in his arms, he gently laid me down on the blanket, his body covering mine. He wiped away my tears and placed a gentle kiss on my lips. "I promise you'll see me again. I'm in love with you, Hadley. I don't want tomorrow to come any more than you do."

He kissed me again, but I gasped and pulled away. "What did you just say?"

Brushing the hair off my face, he smiled and traced my lips with his fingers. "I said I love you." He trailed his lips down my neck. "And I want to make love to you . . . right here. Tonight is all we have."

Blake nipped at my ear. "I bought you something. Hopefully, you'll think of me when you look at it." We'd just made love under the open sky and were snuggling under one of the many blankets he'd brought. He turned and reached over to pull out a small jewelry box from the picnic basket.

Handing it to me, I gasped as I opened it. "Oh wow, it's beautiful." Inside was an amethyst stone necklace, held in place by swirls of diamonds encrusted in the silver lining. He took it out and placed it around my neck. I tried to look down at it, but could barely see it through the tears. "Thank you. I'll wear it every day."

"Even when you're walking the red carpet without me?" he asked flippantly. As much as he joked, I could see the pain in his eyes.

"Yes, even on the red carpet. I want you with me, always. I love you, Blake Evans."

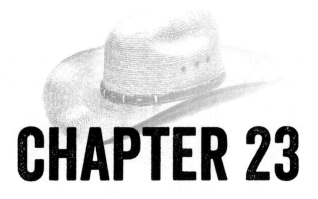

CHAPTER 23

HADLEY

"I think Nightshade's going to miss you," Tyla said, coming up behind me.

Gasping, I turned around, clutching my chest. "Holy hell, I didn't hear you come in."

She smiled and patted Nightshade's back. "You were too busy talking to him to notice. Although, judging by the way Blake is this morning, I'd say this horse isn't the only one who's going to miss you. How did it go last night?"

"Amazing, and I wanted to thank you for that. The food was out of this world. It's almost not fair how you can be so good with horses *and* cooking."

She brushed her shoulders off. "Thank you. I figured

I could help Blake out with his last night with you. I have to say though, it doesn't look like either one of you are happy about this situation."

I glanced over her shoulder at Blake, who'd just walked outside with my bags and the case with his grandfather's guitar in it. "We don't have a choice. I have to go."

"No, you don't. You can always stay here."

Sighing, I shook my head. "If you only knew."

"If I only knew what," she placed her hands on her hips, "that you're Hadley Rivers?"

I froze. "How did you know that?"

She chuckled. "It was quite easy to figure out. You look just like her, minus the makeup, and I caught you singing your songs when you thought no one was listening. Plus, I know what Blake does for a living. When word got out that you were in protective custody, I put it all together."

"You didn't tell anyone did you?"

"Are you kidding? I care about Blake and I admire what he does. I would never jeopardize this for him, or for you." Her gaze landed on Blake. "I've never seen him like this before. He loves you."

"And I love him, but it doesn't change anything. I still have to go back to California."

She snorted. "Why? I'm pretty sure celebrities don't always live in Hollywood. You could stay here and still travel."

"Robert's coming," Blake called.

Sucking in a breath, I heard the car come down the driveway. "And I would've, if he'd asked me to stay. But that hasn't happened." All night, we'd made love to each other, and all night, I waited on him to ask me to stay. That was what hurt the worst. I thought he would; especially after he told me he loved me. The words never came.

Tyla pulled me into a hug and squeezed. "He might not have said it, but he wants it. He'll come to his senses."

A tear fell down my cheek. "I hope so, Tyla. I truly do. Maybe one day, I'll see you again."

"You will."

Taking a deep breath, I let her go and slowly walked up to the front of the house where Blake stood. "I guess this is it," I said, forcing a smile.

He pulled me into his arms, burying his nose against my neck. "Call me when you get home, so I know you got there safely."

I nodded. "I will. Be careful on your mission."

"Always am."

As soon as he let me go, I jumped back in his arms and kissed him hard.

At first, he opened up to me, but then he pulled away and rested his forehead to mine. "You're not making this easy."

"Neither are you," I whispered.

"Hadley?" a voice called.

What the hell? I jerked around to find my father in the driveway beside Robert. "What are you doing here?" He stood there dressed to perfection, in his crisp gray suit and his white hair expertly coifed. My father was worth millions and his appearance reeked of it.

He cleared his throat. "I came to see you home safely." He turned and threw a glare to Blake. "Mr. Evans, I seem to recall paying you to keep her *safe*, not to take advantage of her."

"Wait, *what?*" I turned back to Blake. "What is he talking about?"

Jaw tense, he returned my father's glare. "I would never take advantage of your daughter, sir. So don't come to my house threatening me. You want your money back? Take it, I don't give a flying fuck about the pay."

Robert held up his hands. "All right, that's enough. I'm sure there's an explanation for all of this, but it'll have to be settled at another time. We have a plane to catch. Blake," he said, extending his hand. "It's good to see you again. Thank you for keeping Hadley safe." Blake nodded and shook his hand.

"Hadley, it's time to go," my father commanded.

"In a minute," I growled, anger boiling in my veins. I pushed past Blake and he followed me to the side of the house, out of my father's sight. "Care to tell me what's going on?"

He unclenched his fists. "Yeah, your dad's an ass."

"I know that already. What about the money? How much did he give you?"

Sighing, he lowered his head. "Ten million."

Mouth gaping, I almost choked on my words. "Is that the only reason you agreed to let me stay?"

"Yes." When I tried to walk away, he grabbed my hand and pulled me into his arms. "Don't walk away from me, Hadley. I admit, I didn't want you here in the beginning, but you knew that. I don't care about the money, I care about you. That's why I haven't touched a cent of it. The money isn't what I fell in love with."

I sagged in his arms and let the tears flow. "Then keep it. I'm sure you'll find something to do with it." The horn beeped and I stepped away. "I have to go."

Blake reached for my hand, but I pulled back. "Don't leave like this, Hadley. What do you want me to say?"

"I can't be the one to tell you, you'll have to figure this one out on your own." Turning on my heel, I walked straight past my dad and into the car. Real life wasn't like the movies. I thought for sure he'd scoop me into his arms and beg me to stay. Instead, he let me go and I watched him disappear behind the cloud of dust from our car as we drove away.

"It's good to see you again, sweet pea," my father announced.

Huffing, I turned away from the window and glared at him. "You didn't need to be rude to Blake. He didn't use me for the money."

He sighed. "I know, but getting involved wasn't a good decision on either part. Nothing can come of it."

"Why? Because he's not a celebrity? What does that matter?"

"You've been through this before and I don't want to see you get hurt again. You need someone who can handle the press, and what it's like to be in the public eye. Nick can do that and I know he cares about you. We'll just keep your relationship with Mr. Evans a secret."

I shook my head. "No, Dad. I love Blake and I want to be with him. Once he's done with his mission, he'll come for me."

He blew out a sigh and ran a hand over his weathered face. "Honey, don't you see? He can't be with you and keep his job. What kind of undercover detective would he be if he's in the spotlight? Everyone would know his face. He'll have to give up his career. And even if he was willing, would you let him? He'd resent you in the end."

I glanced at Robert and he nodded. "It's true. Blake won't be able to do his job if he's with you. But it's a decision he'll have to make for himself."

Could I let him give up everything to be with me? I knew the answer, and it felt like a kick to my gut.

CHAPTER 24

BLAKE

(One Week Later)

"What the fuck, Evans? You almost killed him," Mason barked.

I slapped handcuffs on the sick fuck we'd been tracking and dragged him to his feet by yanking on his neck. His face was a bloody mess, but the bastard deserved it after raping and strangling two women because they wouldn't go out with him. I *wanted* to kill him.

"I still can," I snapped back. "Maybe I should cut off his dick and see how he likes that." The guy whimpered and I smacked him across the head. "Shut the fuck up! Hope you enjoy being raped and mutilated in prison because that's exactly what you're going to get."

Mason drove us to the station and I happily tossed the fucker through the front door. If he didn't get out of my sight immediately, it wasn't going to be long before I did something I'd regret.

Mason slapped a hand on my shoulder and pulled me to the side. "Dude, you need to calm the fuck down. I know the guy deserves to get the shit beat out of him, but one more knock to the head could kill him. His punishment isn't done, believe me. Now go outside and calm down. I got this."

Once we were done at the station, we headed back to the hotel to pack our stuff. We'd been in Texas for a week, and during that time, I'd gotten one message from Hadley. I couldn't stop replaying it over in my mind. What made it worse was, she wouldn't return my calls.

"Still haven't heard from her?" Mason asked.

Clenching my teeth, I shoved the rest of my clothes into my duffle. "Nope. But I've seen a lot of pictures of her and her boyfriend floating around the internet."

Mason finished packing and sat down on his bed. "I thought she wasn't dating him."

I huffed. "That's what she said, but every time I search for her on the internet, there's a new picture of them together. It pisses me the fuck off."

"What did her message say? You never told me."

I signed into my voicemail and clicked on her message. "Here you go." I tossed him the phone. It was on speaker, so I could listen to it again. I guess I loved punishing myself.

"Hey, Blake, it's me. I got home safely and it's been nothing but craziness since I got back. So . . . on the way home, I did some thinking. As much as I love you, I just fear that by being with me it'll hold you back. If you're seen with me and people find out who you are, you can't exactly do your undercover work anymore."

She paused and cleared her throat, her voice shaky when she spoke again. *"I'm not going to ask you to give that up for me. I won't. I love you so much, but if I have to let you go, I will. I'll do it for you."*

Mason blew out a long breath. "She has a point. If you go to her, I don't see how you could keep up this life. Are you ready to do that?"

"You didn't give it up. You're an MMA legend and still doing this work. How come you can have the best of both worlds?"

He slapped me on the back and handed me my phone. "Because I'm good at what I do, just like you. But think about it, I can't go undercover anymore. And your face would be in the news all of the time. You'd be relegated to more of a desk job. It's something I'm sure you could pull off, but that's up to you if it's worth it."

Grabbing my bag, I headed for the door. "You're

right. And I know exactly what to do." As I ran down the hall, I dialed Hadley's number. It wasn't a surprise when she didn't answer the phone. *Beep.*

"I don't know why you're not answering my calls, but you will listen to what I have to say, even if I have to rope you in, like I did before. I choose you, Hadley. As long as I have you, nothing else matters. If you don't want me, that's fine, but I want you to say it to my face. I'll be with you soon."

CHAPTER 25

HADLEY

"Hey, babe. What are you doing out here?" Nick asked, elbowing me in the side.

The party was so loud, I'd went outside to catch a break and then realized I'd missed a call from Blake. Tears streamed down my cheeks, but they were happy tears.

"I needed some fresh air." Which was true, but I also wanted to listen to Blake's message. It was exactly what I needed to hear.

"Why are you crying then? Is there something you want to talk about?"

For the past week, I'd ignored Blake's calls, even though I really wanted to answer them. I was afraid he was going to let me go and by not talking to him, I didn't have to hear it. But now I knew he was coming for me, and that meant I had to end the ruse with Nick — breaking his heart in the process.

Taking a deep breath, I turned to him and took his hand. "Nick, you know I care about you, right?"

Sighing, he set his beer down. "You're breaking up with me, aren't you? I knew this was coming."

"Technically, we weren't really going out."

"What happened? Ever since you came back, you've been different. You barely let me touch you."

I nodded. "I know and I'm sorry. I didn't want to tell you on the phone and it's been killing me not to tell you since I've been back. I just hadn't figured everything out yet, and the last thing I wanted to do was hurt you."

He waved me on. "Spit it out, so we can get this over with."

Taking a deep breath, I closed my eyes and let it out slowly. "I met someone."

His eyes widened. "Met someone? Who? You've been in protective custody!" When I didn't answer, he let go of my hand. "Holy fuck, you have to be kidding me. You fell for your *bodyguard*?"

"He's actually an undercover cop. And I didn't want to fall for him, it just happened."

Jaw tense, he shot to his feet. "And does he care about you?"

I sighed. "He loves me, Nick. He's coming for me. Look, I don't want to lose you over this. You're my friend, my *best* friend." Shaking his head, he stormed off through the gardens and disappeared into the darkness. "Nick, wait!"

"What's with all the yellin'?" Tristan asked. He'd walked up to me, followed by Kip and Dawson.

I pointed to where Nick disappeared. "He's pissed at me. Will you guys make sure he doesn't do anything stupid? I know how he gets when he drinks."

Kip laughed. "What did you do, break up with him?" He lifted the beer to his lips and stopped when I glared at him. "Fucking shit, did you?"

I rolled my eyes. "It's a long story, but yes. I don't want him out there, drinking alone. You guys tend to get stupid when you're drunk and angry."

"Maybe *these* assholes," Tristan replied. "I'm playing it sober tonight. Don't worry though, we'll take care of him."

"Thanks, guys. And thank you for helping me move into my apartment. There was no way I could stay at my house after what happened."

Kip and Dawson sandwiched me in a hug. "You're welcome," they said, before letting me go.

Tristan pulled me in next and blew out a sigh. "Do you need a ride?"

"No, I'll be fine. If you hadn't noticed, there's a giant

mammoth of a man watching us from a few yards away. He used to be a fighter in Ireland."

Tristan glanced over my shoulder and chuckled. "I see. Guess your dad wants to make sure you're protected. Looks like a solid choice."

"Yeah, but I don't want to be followed around for the rest of my life."

"You'll get used to it. Sometimes it's for the best."

He hugged me again and Kip whistled. "Come on dude, let's go."

All three guys waved and disappeared into the darkness. My heart hurt for Nick, but I couldn't play pretend with him forever. Hopefully, he would understand.

"Miss Rivers, is it true you ended things with Nick Myers last night? Our sources say you cheated on him. What do you say about that?"

Connor pushed his way through the crowd and growled, "I say you get out of her face, now." His Irish accent was thick and I doubted any of the reporters could tell what he said, but they moved out of his way. It was either that or get trampled. My dad had made sure to pick a bodyguard I wouldn't be interested in.

Mission accomplished.

"Almost through," Connor grunted.

The second I got off the plane in New York, it had been constant badgering about my failed relationship with Nick. Felicity wasn't happy and I could see her fuming every time someone shouted another question at me.

Luckily, the light at the end of the tunnel was near and we were able to get in a car and drive away. "Holy shit, I didn't think it would be *that* bad," I said.

Felicity snorted. "What did you expect? You and Nick were one of the hottest couples in Hollywood. Now every single female in town is going to be after him. I hope you're ready for that."

"I truly just want him happy. If that means he has to sleep with a hundred women, so be it. I'm not holding him back anymore. I'll always be grateful for what he did for me."

Leaning her head against the seat, she closed her eyes. "He was just so upset when I talked to him last night. It breaks my heart, Hadley."

"Mine too, but I couldn't pretend forever. I don't love him, and I realize that now. Falling in love with Blake has opened my eyes. Nick will be happier in the end. You'll see."

"I sure hope so. When did Blake say he was coming to see you?"

Shrugging, I looked down at my phone. "I don't

know. He just said he was coming." But I didn't know if Blake knew how to find me, since I'd given back my untraceable cell. Every time I called him, it went straight to voicemail. I hadn't actually talked to him since I left Wyoming.

The concert at Madison Square Garden was in a couple of hours, and Connor was driving us there for warm ups. I was nervous to get on stage. It'd only been a day since I'd told Nick about Blake, and the media couldn't wait to slap a big, red *A* on my chest.

CHAPTER 26

HADLEY

"Thank you, everyone!" I shouted, waving at the crowd. It felt good to be on stage again. The adrenaline flowed through my veins and I soaked it all in. I blew a kiss to the fans and rushed off stage.

"Hot damn, you were on fire," Felicity exclaimed, handing me a towel and a bottle of water.

Laughing, I wiped the sweat off my brow. "Thanks. I forgot how much fun it was to perform."

"You definitely haven't lost your touch. In fact, I think you've gotten better, bolder even."

"Has Blake called?"

She passed me my phone. "No, but he texted and said he was getting on a plane for New York. He'll be in late tonight. I replied and gave him the name of the hotel you're staying at."

Squealing, I jumped up and down. "I can't wait for you to meet him."

She gave me a sad smile as she stared at something over my shoulder. "There's someone who wants to see you." She squeezed my arm and I froze. I knew who was there, and I didn't know if I was ready to see him so soon. "I'll give you two some privacy. Because once you walk out those doors over there," she said, pointing to the exit, "you're going to be bombarded with reporters. They know he's back here."

As soon as she walked off, I could feel him come up behind me.

"You did great tonight."

My chest tightened, but I held back the tears as I turned to face him. "Were you here the whole time?"

He ran a hand through his midnight colored hair and smiled. I could tell it was forced. "I didn't want to miss your first time back. I knew you'd be nervous as hell."

I snorted. "You got that right. I guess I didn't think you'd want to see me after last night."

Sighing, he pulled me into his arms. "I'm not gonna lie, I was pissed. But I also know you weren't mine to begin with." He tilted my chin up, his soft green gaze focusing on mine. "You've been nothing but honest with me along the way, and I was just too hardheaded to listen. Which is why I went to the press and told them we ended things amicably. I saw what they were posting about you and I didn't like it. Your reputation didn't need to be trashed because of me."

"Nick, you didn't have to do that."

"Yes, I did," he murmured. "I guess now I can enjoy the single life for a while."

We stepped away from each other and I could feel the distance between us. It would always be different from this point on. "Please tell me I haven't lost you as a friend. I care about you, Nick. You mean a lot to me."

"I'm not going anywhere, Hadley. It might take some time for me to get adjusted, but we'll get there. If you want, you can come out with me and the guys tonight. I think Felicity's coming."

I shook my head. "I think I'll just go back to the hotel and crash. I'm heading back to California tomorrow."

He nodded, then his gaze landed on the stage door. "Want me to go out there with you?"

The crowd of reporters could be heard through the door. "No, I got it. Thank you though. I'm sure Connor will get me through pretty fast. I'll see you back in California, okay?"

He nodded. "Goodbye, Hadley."

"Bye, Nick." I kissed his cheek and started for the door, where Connor stood.

"You ready?" he asked.

Taking a deep breath, I let it out slowly. "Yep. Let's go." He opened the door and I stepped out into the madness.

"Miss Rivers, are you and Nick going to work things out? We know he was backstage with you," a female reporter shouted, shoving a microphone in my face.

"We're friends, and we always will be," I replied. Connor nudged me to keep moving.

"Are you seeing someone else? Who is he?" another reporter asked.

"I think that's enough questions for tonight," Connor announced.

"Mr. MacCabe, how do you feel knowing Miss Rivers' last bodyguard was shot and killed on duty?"

Huffing, he turned around and blocked me from view. There were two security guards by the back door and they rushed up and blocked the reporters from going any further. Connor opened the back door and ushered me into the car. He watched me clasp the buckle and then pointed at something in the center console. "I was told you liked ginger ale. I got you a bottle and put it in there."

"Oh, thank you." I opened the bucket and pulled out the chilled bottle as he walked around front and got into the driver's seat. "Do you want some?" I asked, holding out a bottle.

He shook his head. "Trying to watch my figure."

I snorted at his response. Opening my own bottle, I chugged half of it and sat back relaxed. "What time do you think we'll make it back to the hotel?"

"Fifteen minutes, probably. Lots of traffic."

Pulling out my phone, I saw where Felicity had texted him back. I couldn't wait to see him.

Me: I'll be at the hotel in 15 mins. Meet in lobby?

Blake: See you there.

The traffic went to a standstill and Connor swerved around, taking another street.

"What are you doing?" I asked.

"Shortcut. Do you still have your seatbelt on?"

Everything started to get blurry and my eyes grew heavy. "Yeah, I . . . I think . . . so." My words sounded like they were jumbled together. I grabbed the strap and felt it across my chest, my fingers tingling as I clutched it. "Connor, I don't feel so good."

"What's wrong? Do I need to stop the car?"

My whole body started to go numb and I couldn't speak. It was as if my mind was still there, but only not. Time didn't seem to exist. The car picked up speed and everything went black. Connor yelled for me to hold on, but I couldn't feel my hands and my muscles weren't listening to my brain's warning to grasp onto something. All I could feel was the heat of flames across my skin, yet there was no pain.

CHAPTER 27

BLAKE

"What the fuck is going on?" I grumbled. Hadley had sent me a text hours ago saying she was on her way to the hotel. Where the hell was she? The hotel staff hadn't seen her come in and she wasn't in her room. I texted and called, but no reply.

My phone rang and I picked it up. "Where are you?" I barked into the phone, thinking it was her.

"I'm in California." It was Robert and he sounded hesitant.

"Shit. Sorry, Robert. I thought you were Hadley. What's going on?"

"Are you in New York?"

"Yeah, I just got here."

His heavy sigh made me tense. "I think you should go to the station. There's been an accident."

"Accident? What kind of accident?"

"Look at the news and you'll see. I'm sorry, Blake. I didn't want to be the one to tell you."

Dropping my phone, I ran into the hotel bar and pushed past everyone crowded around the counter. The TV's above showed nothing but fire, and the words below emblazoned in blue, *Hadley Rivers, dead?*

Holy fuck.

Women around me cried while others watched the news in complete horror. I couldn't watch anymore. "She's dead?" someone cried. "How can she be dead? Wasn't she just giving a concert tonight? She was so young."

I refused to believe it. She wasn't gone, it had to be a mistake. *What if it wasn't?*

"Fuck." I gripped the counter and momentarily felt lightheaded before the anger took over. If it was her in that car, someone was going to pay for taking her away from me. Growling, I hurried back to where I dropped my phone, dialing Robert's number as I stormed out the door.

"Evan's, you okay?"

"Call the Chief of Police out here and tell them I'm coming."

"What are you going to do? You can't interfere in

this."

"I don't care. I want answers." Everything inside of me was numb. I didn't want to feel the pain yet. I wanted answers, and I sure as hell was going to get them.

"I'm sorry Mr. Evans, but I can't allow you back there. The chief said only family is allowed at this time." The arrogant twat glanced down at his paperwork, completely dismissing me.

My blood boiled. I'd been sitting there for over two fucking hours. "Look, fucker," I growled, grabbing him by the neck, "I showed you my badge and told you who I am. I want to talk to the Chief of Police. I suggest you let me back there before I rip off your goddamn head." He grasped at my hands, but all it did was make me squeeze harder.

"Mr. Evans, let him go. I'm Byron Jennings." I glanced over my shoulder at the middle-aged man, pursing his lips. "Robert called and told me to expect you." He had graying, dark hair and a moustache, his uniform badge confirming he was the Chief of Police.

I squeezed shitdick's neck one more time because it felt good, and then let him go. He grabbed his neck and fell back in his chair, coughing.

Byron stood to the side and motioned for me to walk

past. "I'd appreciate it if you didn't assault my staff."

"And I'd appreciate it if he wouldn't act like a cunt. Now what happened to Hadley?"

Sighing, he started down the hall and I followed. "It looks like her bodyguard lost control of the car. They slammed into a tree right outside of Burnsville. According to her agent, she was staying at a hotel in town. It makes no sense why they were heading out of the city."

Where the hell was she going? "Something's not right. She sent me a text right after her concert saying she was on her way to the hotel. There's no fucking way this was an accident."

He shrugged. "We don't have any evidence proving otherwise. Hadley's father did say he'd received threats on her life over the past couple of years, but as far as we can tell, they were all just ploys to get his money. Believe me, if this was intentional, we'll find the culprit. Right now, we have our people gathering everything they can. As it stands, it's being ruled as an accident . . ."

Byron's mouth kept moving, but I couldn't hear a fucking thing he said.

The signs were there . . . why couldn't anyone else see it as I did? It wasn't a fucking accident. My chest tightened so hard, I could barely draw in a breath. I didn't want to feel the pain of her loss; I wanted the anger. It didn't hurt as bad if I could focus on that. Every time I closed my eyes, I saw her face. I should've been there to protect her. If I'd only gotten to her sooner.

"Mr. Evans, stop!" The voice seemed so far away. I could feel arms drawing me back. There was blood dripping from my right hand and a large hole in the wall. There was a larger hole in my chest. "What the fuck is your problem?" Byron shouted.

I collapsed into the wall and looked down at my hands. They were blurry and my eyes burned. I never fucking cried. The cops in front of me watched my every move, as if I was going to snap.

"I'll pay for the damage," I said, not even recognizing the voice that came out of my mouth. I didn't feel like myself anymore.

"Guys, back off," Byron commanded. The cops scattered, but chose to stay close just in case. I couldn't blame them. I was a ticking time bomb. The chief approached me cautiously and placed a hand on my shoulder. "Robert told me you two were involved. I'm sorry, I know this is difficult. But I can't help you if you don't calm down."

"Tell me the rest."

"From what we can piece together, after the crash, the car burst into flames. There didn't appear to be a struggle to get out."

The thought of Hadley burning to death made me sick. Swallowing hard, I nodded and blew out a shaky breath. "How fast were they going?"

"Judging by the damage, it was probably around twenty miles per hour. There were skid marks found at the scene, where they swerved off the road. You're more than welcome to look at what we have so far. We've also recovered a couple of Hadley's belongings."

Jaw tense, I nodded. "I want to see them."

He led me further down the hall and I stopped in front of one of the doors. I recognized the guy inside. It was Nick, and he had his arm around another female, who sat sobbing uncontrollably.

Byron nodded to them. "That's Hadley's agent, Felicity, and her brother, Nick. He and Hadley were involved for a time."

"I know." Even though it was all a ploy, I didn't bother correcting him. It was no use. I was the last person Nick would want to see.

"All right, let's go in here." Byron opened the door to the next room. There was nothing in there but a table and four chairs. "Have a seat and I'll get everything we've gathered so far." I walked inside and paced the floor to keep my body moving. If I slowed down, I'd crash. A few minutes later, Byron walked in with two file folders and a box, placing them on the table. "Do you need some privacy?"

"Please," I replied. He nodded once and shut the door on his way out.

I slid the folders toward me and didn't bother with the box. I wasn't ready to see its contents. I'd never been so scared to open a file in my life. Taking a deep breath, I opened the first folder and read everything from start to finish.

There were no witnesses to see what'd actually happened. I didn't like that at all.

Pushing the folder away, I stared down at the next one containing pictures. I carefully opened it up and closed my eyes when the first picture came into view. It was of the back of the car, all black and charred from fire. Bile burned my throat as I flipped to the next picture; the backseat, with nothing but a pile of ash. To be burnt like that, the car had to have been on fire for quite a while.

Closing my eyes, I slammed my fist on the table. "Fuck, fuck, fuck."

I pushed the pictures away and my hand grazed across the box. If I couldn't look at another picture, how the hell was I going to look in the box? My body shook and I was ready to explode, but I didn't know what to do. For the first time in my life, I was lost.

Taking a deep breath, I reached for the box and opened it. Everything was covered in a black film. There was one thing that stuck out at me above the rest. I pulled it out and wiped it off with my shirt. Gritting my teeth, I clenched the crystal so hard in my fist it drew blood. It was all that was left of the necklace I'd given

Hadley; it was all that was left of her period.

The door to the room opened and Byron cleared his throat.

Lifting my head, I wiped the tears angrily away from my face. "I've seen shit like this for years and it's never bothered me before."

He took the seat across from me. "I know. My brother was shot in an armed robbery call. It was the hardest thing I've ever witnessed."

How the hell could he compare Hadley's situation to that? "Speaking of witnesses, why aren't there any? Someone had to have seen something."

"We're working on it. They were in the middle of nowhere when it happened. There's nothing we could find that would suggest foul play."

Growling, I pounded a hand on the table and stood. "*Everything* points to that," I shouted. "They weren't where they were supposed to be and they ended up dead. If your people can't figure this shit out, I'll do it myself." Storming to the door, I slammed it open and walked out, only to run right into Felicity and Nick.

Felicity's eyes went wide and she gasped. "Blake?" she cried.

Nick tensed, recognition flaring in his gaze. I was the one who took Hadley from him, and now she was gone forever. All that was left of her was the crystal I had fisted in my hand.

"I know you cared about her," Byron called, "but there's nothing you can do. She's gone. Killing yourself over this case will only make it worse."

I glanced over my shoulder. "I don't care. Something's not right and I'm going to figure it out. I'm not letting this go." Without another word, I turned and headed for the exit. But I wasn't alone. Nick's footsteps pounded heavily behind me.

"Hey," he ordered. I ignored him and walked out into the parking lot to the black SUV I'd rented. "Hey, I'm talking to you," he shouted angrily.

Stopping at the car, I jerked around, fists clenched at my sides. "And I'm telling you to leave me the fuck alone."

He held his hands up. "I'm not trying to start shit. I just want to know what's going on. They haven't told me anything because I'm not family."

I scoffed. "What's there to say? Hadley's dead. She's fucking *gone*!"

His eyes blazed. "Don't you think I know that? She might've chosen you, but I've known her a whole hell of a lot longer. That's why I want to help."

"*You*, help *me*? That's a joke, right?"

"Call it whatever you want, but you said it yourself, something's not right. I can feel it in my bones. She was supposed to go to the hotel, not head north. Why the fuck was she heading out of the city?"

I threw my hands in the air. "Fuck if I know, but I'm going to find out."

"And I'm going to help you," he offered.

"No, you're not," I snapped, getting into the car. "I work alone. What I do is dangerous. It's not like the figure skating bullshit you do on the ice." I didn't even hear his retort because I slammed the door in his face and tore out of the parking lot. I wasn't going to rest until I found out what happened to Hadley.

CHAPTER 28

BLAKE

"Are you doing okay?" Logan asked. "Robert told me everything. I can't believe this shit."

I gripped the steering wheel so hard, my knuckles turned white. "It's like a fucking nightmare I can't get out of. I had to get wasted just to get through the night."

"I understand, brother. Hadley was an amazing woman. Where are you headed now?"

"Burnsville. I'm going to see what I can find. I just want to know what happened, and the fucknuts here seem to be satisfied with calling this an accident." I was only ten miles away and the closer I got, the more I felt the weight of her loss.

"Is there anything I can do? Your resources are

probably limited, being away from home."

"I brought my laptop, but I was too drunk last night to do anything. Do you mind tapping into the satellite feeds and see if you can find any kind of video of what happened? I need to see the accident."

He typed away on his computer. "On it. I'll give you a call back."

"Thanks."

We hung up and I concentrated on the road. Burnsville was a small, Sleepy Hollow type of town. It was so miniscule, no one had ever heard of it. The crash site was easy to spot with all the flowers, charred ground, and yellow tape. I didn't want to imagine Hadley's life ending there, but it was staring at me, right in the fucking face. There was no goodbye, or one last touch. She was simply . . . gone.

As soon as I got out of the car, all I could do was stand there. My feet wouldn't take me any closer. I thought I could handle it, but I was wrong. Dropping to my knees, I punched the blackened ground, over and over. The throbbing ache in my chest was almost too much for me to take.

Placing my hands on the ground, I closed my eyes and squeezed them tight, trying to hold back the tears. "I'm sorry, Hadley. I'm so fucking sorry."

A car door slammed and the sadness turned to rage. Why couldn't I have one fucking minute to think without someone interrupting me? Getting to my feet, I swiped at my eyes and turned around. "What are you doing here?" I growled, glaring at the inconsiderate cocksucker headed my way.

Nick sighed and approached cautiously. "I followed you. I told you I wanted to help. Plus, I think there's some things you need to know." His gaze landed on the charred ground and he froze. "I didn't realize how hard it was going to be to come here." Tears flooded his eyes and he cleared his throat, looking away.

I snapped my fingers in front of his face, drawing him back. "Focus! What do I need to know?"

"I was at the station this morning and Mr. Rivers was there. I overheard him on the phone saying he was leaving for a couple of days but he'd be back for the funeral. Why would he be leaving when his daughter was just killed?"

"Fuck if I know. He's a busy man."

His brows furrowed and he shook his head. "Too busy to grieve over his own daughter? No. It's strange. He's not exactly acting like a father who just lost his daughter."

"What exactly are you saying?"

He shrugged. "I think you might be right. Something about Hadley's death is wrong and I don't like how everyone's brushing it off as an accident. I heard some of the guys at the station say you're one of the best undercover cops around. Is that true?"

Turning on my heel, I stormed back to the car and opened the door. "If I was, this never would've happened."

"Then let's figure this shit out."

"Don't you need to go take care of your sister and handle the paparazzi or something?"

His jaw clenched. "Stop being a dick and let me help you. I've known her for years and if I'm able to help in even the smallest capacity, isn't it worth keeping me around?"

We stared each other down, but I could see the determination in his eyes. He loved her too. "Fine. Get in my way and I'll break both your legs. Let's see how you play hockey then." I got in my car, and of course, fuckhead followed me to the motel; it was the only one in the small town. One thing was for sure, I wasn't leaving until I had my answers.

"Are you going to be up my ass the entire time?" I opened the door to my room and Nick brushed past me.

"Have you heard anything?"

"No, I haven't. It's been three hours. Now calm the fuck down." I slammed the door and sat back down at my computer.

Blowing out an angry breath, he ran his hands through his hair and paced. "I'm trying. I don't see how you're all calm about this."

I glared at him. "I'm calm because I have to be. I can't do my job being irrational and angry." I wanted to be angry and beat the shit out of things, but I couldn't.

Nick sat on the bed and lowered his head. "I just never thought she'd be taken away from me."

I sighed and turned my gaze back to the screen. All of the pictures Hadley took in Wyoming were saved to my computer. I couldn't stop looking at them, at her. "Neither did I," I murmured.

For the next hour, I searched through everything I could find on George Rivers' whereabouts. I called his office and all they would say was that he was out of town for a couple of days. There wasn't much to go on, especially since he hadn't paid for anything with any of his credit cards recently, so I could track his location. There was, however, a sum of five million dollars taken out of his bank two days ago, the day Hadley was killed.

"What are you up to, George?" I mumbled at the screen.

"What do you mean?" Nick asked.

I'd been completely engrossed in my work and forgotten he was in the room. I pointed at the screen and he walked over. "You see this? That's five million dollars taken out of George Rivers' account two days ago. Why the hell would he need that much money?"

Nick shook his head. "Have you figured out where he's at?"

"Not yet. I'm trying to tap into his phone to see if I can locate him that way. It just takes time. Once I link in, all we'll have to do is wait." I typed in the information and waited for the wheel of death to stop spinning. Nick watched on in fascination and we both breathed a sigh of relief when my software synced with George's phone. I knew it would, but being in the middle of a desolate town, I figured it'd take longer.

"How long do we have to wait?"

"I don't know," I answered with a shrug. "It depends on how far away he is. Once we find him, hopefully, it'll give us an idea of what he's up to."

"You don't think he had anything to do with the accident do you? He was always so overly protective of Hadley."

"You're right. I don't believe he would ever purposely hurt her. I just want to know what he's up to."

I clicked over to another screen where a picture of her working in the barn popped up. She wasn't looking when I'd taken it, but I had to have proof that I'd gotten her to shovel shit. She would've killed me if she knew I took it.

"Is that Hadley?" Nick asked. Nodding, I turned the

computer toward him. His eyes lit up when he looked at her. "What is she doing?"

Chuckling, I pointed at her picture. "Shoveling shit. When she first came out to Wyoming, I didn't want her there. I thought it was an insult to my talent to have to babysit a spoiled Hollywood brat."

"She was never like that," he snapped.

I held up my hand. "I know, but it took a while for me to see. Anyway, I made her sweep out the stalls and help me in the barn. She turned out to be one hell of a rider. Nightshade loved her."

"I went about it all wrong," he grumbled. "Who would've thought she'd want a guy who made her clean up horse shit?"

The memories made me laugh. "My thought exactly."

A sad smile spread across his face. "Do you mind if I scroll through the pictures? I've never seen her like this."

I nodded and turned the computer toward him. He burst out laughing when he saw the pictures of me in the Mexican pointy boots. I didn't want to think about what it was going to be like getting on a plane and going home without her.

A phone rang. My pulse spiked when I saw who it was. "Logan. Got any news?"

"Do I ever," he exclaimed. "Are you sitting down?"

CHAPTER 29

HADLEY

Cinnamon apples. I loved the smell of cinnamon apples so much that I had a candle in every room of my house. Was I home? How could that be? Footsteps sounded on the hardwood floor below me, but I wasn't the one doing the walking. A set of arms held me tight and I sighed, thinking it was Blake but the cologne was different. I recognized it.

"Connor?"

"It's me. I'm moving you to a different room," he murmured. Ever so slowly, I could finally move my arms and my legs. My muscles ached across my chest; especially when Connor laid me down in the bed. By the time I could open my eyes, I watched him walk out the door.

"You're awake," a voice called out to my right.

Groaning, I turned my head to the side. "Dad?"

He smiled at me and grabbed my hand. "How do you feel?"

"Like I've been run over by a train. What happened?" I glanced down at my arm where a bandage covered the inside of my elbow.

My father glanced down at my arm and cleared his throat. "You were in an accident. They just took you off the IV."

"Where am I?" It looked like a house instead of a hospital. A really nice house, as a matter of fact.

"Connor brought you here and had a private physician check you out. We didn't want the media attention. They can't touch you here."

"Accident? What kind of accident? I can't remember anything." All I could remember was being in the car and then . . . nothing.

He squeezed my hand and stood. "Connor lost control of the car and ran off the road. He's fine and so are you."

"Where are we?"

For a split second, he hesitated and then answered. "In Canada. Connor knew you'd be safe up here."

"Canada," I shouted incredulously. "That makes no sense. Where's Blake? He was coming for me. I have to let him know where I am."

"Shh, it's okay," he uttered gently, kneeling down by the bed. "Blake knows where you're at. The media is following him around, hoping he'll come to you. Don't worry, you'll see him soon."

I glanced around the room. "Where's my phone? I need to call him."

"It was lost in the accident. We'll get you another one."

"I can use yours," I said, holding out my hand. "I don't care if the media is following him around or not, he can still talk to me on the phone."

Sighing, he leaned over and kissed me on the head. "My phone's in the car. I have to head back to New York for a bit. I'll be back tomorrow."

"How long do I have to stay here?"

He smiled and I could see a hint of tears in his eyes. Something was wrong. "Just for a few more days."

"Dad, what's wrong? You're keeping something from me."

He shook his head. "It'll all work out in the end. But right now, I have to go. Connor and his people will take care of you." Turning on his heel, he hurried to the door and rushed out.

"Dad, wait!"

He didn't answer. He was gone.

There was a feeling in my gut I couldn't shake. Trees

surrounded the house and there was nothing around from what I could tell. Where the hell was I? Not to mention, there was no phone in the room. I had to call Blake.

Stumbling over to the closet, I opened it up to find an entire wardrobe in my size. Even the bathroom was stocked with the same toiletries I used. Instead of changing clothes, I walked out of the room in my hospital nightgown, and ventured downstairs. The house was enormous and nothing like I'd imagine Connor living in.

"Hadley, what are you doing?"

Gasping, I turned around and grabbed my chest. Connor stood there, dressed in a suit with a gun in his waistband. Why was he carrying a gun in here? "Why aren't you all sore and feeling like shit like I am? You were in the car with me."

He chuckled. "I'm not a woman."

"Ha-ha, very funny," I retorted, glancing around the house. There were pictures on the wall, expensive pieces of artwork.

"You have clothes in your room if you wanted to change. The stuff in the bathroom is yours too. Your father made sure we had everything you needed." That answered one of my questions. "Are you hungry?" he asked.

I nodded. "I feel like I haven't eaten in days."

"You haven't. Why don't you go upstairs to change, and I'll get you something to eat. Meet me down in the gardens and we'll picnic outside." He pointed to a glass door off to the side. I could see the flowers in the garden. They were beautiful.

"Can you bring a phone as well? Dad said mine is gone and there's not one in the room. I need to make a few calls."

"He called everyone, Hadley. My job is to keep you stress-free. The last thing you need to do is worry about everyone else."

Dread settled into the pit of my stomach. I got the feeling they were keeping me away for a reason. Why was I meeting such resistance over a stupid phone call? "I just want to call Blake. That's it. He's probably worried sick about me."

He pointed to the stairs. "After dinner. Now get dressed. You look like you could use a glass of wine."

I wanted to argue but he walked away, leaving me by myself in the large foyer. I hurried up the stairs back to my room. Why did I have so many pairs of clothes? I changed into a pair of shorts and a T-shirt and slowly made my way to the gardens.

There was a gate off to the side that led to the front of the house. Since Connor wasn't out there, I decided to explore. The house was huge, much larger than my father's. A car door slammed out front so I hurried down the sidewalk to see who it was. I would've given anything to see Blake. Before I could turn the corner, a man dressed in a dark gray suit with slicked back brown hair and shades stepped in my way.

"Aren't you supposed to be in the gardens?" he stated matter-of-factly. He was Irish, judging by the accent.

I could feel his penetrating glare through the glasses; it made me uneasy. Crossing my arms over my chest, I stood firm. "Am I not allowed to look around?"

"You are, but I believe it'd be in your best interest to keep an escort."

"Am I in prison?" I snapped.

"No, and I'd be more than happy to assist you in anywhere you want to go."

"I don't think that's necessary," Connor spoke up. He grasped my elbow and pulled me into his side. "Let's go, Hadley." I went with him willingly and glanced over my shoulder at the other guy who turned and headed back to the front of the house.

"What was that about?" I inquired, not wanting to run into that guy anytime soon.

"I suggest you stay away from him."

"Why?"

"He's not as nice as me. Now let's eat." Back in the gardens, there was a whole spread on a table—from roasted chicken and potatoes to a strawberry salad.

There were even chocolate covered bananas.

"Who cooked the food? I must give my compliments. They fixed some of my favorites."

He pulled out my chair and I sat down. "Her name is Ingrid. I told her what you liked and she fixed it," he added, taking the seat across from me.

I ate all my food, along with a couple of extra bananas I really didn't need. I watched Connor eat and he deliberately avoided my stare. "When are you going to stop feeding me bullshit, Connor?"

His head jerked up. "What are you talking about?"

I guzzled down the glass of wine and chuckled. "You know what I'm talking about. I'm fine and I'm ready to go home. I don't want to be here, in some backwoods paradise. Shades said it wasn't a prison, but it sure as hell feels like one."

Sighing, he poured me another glass of wine. "It's not a prison, Hadley. Whatever you want, we can give you. There aren't any bars covering your windows are there?"

I glanced up at the house and snorted. "Probably because there's a security system."

By the look on his face, I was right. "You're more than welcome to move about freely. I'll take you anywhere you want to go. There's even a library here." Grabbing my wine, I got to my feet and almost lost my footing, but Connor caught me. "What the hell? You only drank one glass." He took my glass and set it down on the table.

"I feel . . . strange. My whole body tingles," I slurred. The feeling was familiar, like how'd I'd felt the night of the accident.

"Fuck me," he growled, picking me up in his arms. He carried me inside and up the stairs.

"You drugged me," I hissed angrily. "Why?"

Everything sounded so far away, yet I heard voices all around me. I wanted to scream, to demand to know what was going on. Connor laid me down and the feel of soft satin sheets wrapped around me. My eyes closed and I couldn't feel my body.

"Why the fuck did you drug her?" Connor growled.

"She was asking too many questions." The sound of the voice was oddly familiar, but the accent threw me off.

"Of course, she's going to ask questions. You've known Hadley for how long now? She'll be pissed when she finds out."

The other guy snorted. "She can blame that on her father. Besides, once we get to Ireland and she see's everything I can give her, she'll be all mine."

I was in a dream. There was no way what I was hearing was real. The fogginess started to close in and I could feel myself slipping away. I struggled to stay lucid enough to hear more.

"What the hell are you talking about?" Connor spat. "That was never part of the deal. She doesn't belong to you."

"Nor you, my friend. You're getting too close to her and I don't like it. When we get back home, I want you to stay away from her."

Connor growled low in his chest. "Have you forgotten who you're talking to? I will do whatever the fuck I want. She'll hate you after she finds out what you did."

"Nonsense. Once she finds out her lover is dead, she'll be ready to leave the country. I'll be there to fill the void, and anything else that needs filling." He chuckled.

"But he's not dead."

"Yet."

"What did you do?"

"Let's just say, I have Dillon taking care of it. It'll be a shame when loverboy doesn't make it out alive."

I wanted to scream and cry, but I was a prisoner in my own body. Blake needed my help, and there was no way I could help him. The only thing I knew was, when I woke up in the morning, he could be gone.

CHAPTER 30

BLAKE

"Fuck me," I growled. By the time the tracker linked up to George's phone, he was on the move and heading south to New York.

"Where do you think he was?" Nick asked.

I shrugged. "I don't know, somewhere north of here. Maybe Canada? I'm checking his credit cards to see if he purchased anything in the past two hours." I searched and couldn't find a fucking thing. He was probably paying in cash. *Smart bastard.*

Logan was running a background on Connor MacCabe and so was I. His files were hard to find, immediately causing red flags to go up. The only people who had secret lives were people in the government, or people with enough power to hide what they do. Those were the ones you didn't want to fuck with, but I'd take down anyone who stood between me and Hadley.

Nick pulled up a chair. "Any luck?"

"I'm getting there. Just a few more clicks and I think I'll have it." Searching through the government database was tricky. There were all sorts of codes you had to enter to access everything. They made it that way so others couldn't hack in and get the information. Only one more code and I'd be in. "Okay, here we go."

His file came up, but before I could read anything, my phone rang. It was across the room, connected to the charger.

"Keep reading, I'll get it," Nick offered. Rushing over, he grabbed my phone and froze, mouth gaping.

"What the hell are you doing? Give me the phone." I stood up and made my way across the room.

"It—it's Hadley," he stuttered, quickly handing me the phone.

Heart racing, I swiped my finger across the screen. "Hello?" I wanted to hear Hadley's voice, but that wasn't what I got.

"Be ready. They're coming for you," the caller replied.

"What the fuck are you talking about? Why do you have Hadley's phone? Where is she?"

"No time to explain. If you're still alive tomorrow,

I'll let you know more." He hung up and that was it.

Nick lifted his hands in the air. "Who was it? What was that about?"

I set the phone down and rushed over to my bag. "Looks like we're gonna have some company. Hope you're ready." In my bag, I had my gun and several magazine clips. The second I pulled it out, Nick's eyes went wide.

"You've gotta be shitting me. Who's coming for us?"

"I'm about to find out. Kill the lights." He turned off the lights and I hurried over to my laptop. Connor's file popped up and I searched through it as fast as I could. "Dammit to hell," I groaned.

"What? What do you see?" Nick demanded, hissing low.

I turned the laptop toward him. "Connor's part of the Irish mafia. Everything just got fifty thousand times more difficult."

"I don't understand. Why would George hire one of them to be Hadley's bodyguard?"

"I don't know, but if George pissed them off in any way, they'll use her to get back at him. I know what those guys are capable of." I'd seen some of the people they'd killed over the years. Their tactics were brutal. If they so much as hurt Hadley, I'd spend the rest of my days hunting them all down.

Nick peeked out the window. "And they're coming

to kill us? How did they know we were here?"

"They're good at what they do, that's why."

"What are we going to do? Do you have a plan?"

I glanced at the bed and smiled. "I do, but we have to hurry."

"Why did the light go out?" Nick whispered from his location in the closet.

"They're here." After we'd made the bed look like a body was in it, we took up our posts and waited for over two hours.

Now the time had come. I peeked through the curtains, and luckily, there was only one guy cloaked in darkness. He had his gun out and was attaching a silencer to it.

"How many are there?" Nick whispered through the closet door.

"Just one. He's coming now." I flattened myself up against the wall. Gun in hand, I took a deep breath. As soon as I heard the little click inside the door, it was time.

The door steadily moved open and there was no sound at all. The guy was good. He pointed the gun toward the bed and before he could shoot, I kicked his knees in and heard them crack as he fell to the floor with a grunt.

When he dropped the gun, Nick bolted out of the closet and lunged for it. "Got it," he said, pointing it at the intruder.

I'd half expected him to cower in the closet, but he proved me wrong. "Keep it pointed at him. If he moves, shoot him." The guy's legs were splayed at an odd angle. He wasn't going anywhere anytime soon.

I grabbed his feet and he hissed as I tied him up. When I turned him over, I recognized him immediately from the video. He was the one who helped Connor stage the accident. He was a big guy with long brown hair and a scar under his right eye. There was nothing but death in those eyes.

"Who are you?" I asked.

"I'm not telling you a fucking thing," he snarled. I could barely tell what he said because of his thick, Irish accent.

"Didn't think so." I reared back and punched him hard across the cheek. Blood spurt out of his mouth, along with a tooth. I knew he wouldn't speak and I was banking on that. He was going to suffer.

"Damn," Nick exclaimed. "That shit was hard core."

"I'm just getting started." Resting my boot on one of Scar's broken legs, he winced when I pressed down. "Still no answer?" I goaded.

He didn't give me as much as a groan. The fucker

wasn't going to ever walk again, once I got done with him.

As hard as I could, I jumped on his legs with all my weight. He screamed in pain, but I didn't stop. My knuckles hurt from punching him. I could barely recognize him once I was done. There was blood everywhere, but I wasn't ready to quit. If they were going to fuck with me, I wanted them to see I could fight back. Grabbing him by the neck, I squeezed and listened to him choke.

"Blake, stop! You don't want to kill him," Nick shouted.

"Why not? He was going to kill us. I think it's only fair."

"Uh, I think you've done worse than kill him. The fucker's not going to be able to walk probably ever. His bones are shattered."

Closing my eyes, I took a deep breath and let him go. His head fell to the floor with a loud thump. His body had to be in shock from all the pain. "I need to call in backup. We have to get out of here." I washed up quickly and then dialed Mason's number. He had contacts everywhere.

"Evans, what's up?" he answered.

"If I had the time to tell you, you'd probably shit a brick."

"That bad, huh? I heard about Hadley. I'm sorry,

brother."

Rushing over to the computer, I pulled Connor's file back up. "That's just it. She's alive, Mason. And I need your help."

"Alive? Her funeral is tomorrow. It's all the media can talk about."

"I know you think I'm crazy, but I've been working with Logan on getting some footage, and I saw the accident. It was staged. Hadley's out there somewhere and I'm going to find her. She's being held by the Irish mafia."

He choked and barked out a cough. "Are you fucking kidding me? How did she get involved with them?"

"I think her father has something to do with it. But right now, I'm in Burnsville with a half-dead body in my motel room. They sent one of their goons to kill me. I need you to contact some of your people and get them here as soon as you can."

"All right, I'm on it. I know some guys who can probably be out there within the hour."

"Good. And do me a favor, don't tell anyone Hadley's still alive. Someone wants us to think she's dead and we need to keep it that way. I'm trying to find out where she is and I think I might be close. Her bodyguard is with her. His name is Connor MacCabe."

Mason blew out a sigh. "I'll give my people a call and search for this MacCabe. Good work, Evans."

We hung up and I concentrated on the screen. Nick sat on the bed, sneaking side glances at me. "Something you need to say?" I inquired.

"Not really. I'm just sitting here like it's normal to be around a dead body."

"He's not dead yet, but I'm sure he wishes he was. You get used to seeing shit like this in my line of work. Sometimes it's much worse." There were things I'd seen that still gave me nightmares.

Looking at Connor's file, I found his address in Canada and wrote it down. He'd been in North America for only two years. What made him come here from Ireland? There were several profiles attached to his and it was all people he was connected to, including the ass fuck on the floor — Flynn Dillon. He moved his head and groaned.

"I hope it was worth it, cocksucker. All you had to do was tell me your name. Looks like I had it all along," I spat.

"Who is he?" Nick asked.

"Flynn Dillon. Apparently, he lives in Canada too. I'm seeing a trend here. I guess we know where we need to go."

Nick pulled out his phone. "My best friend lives just across the border. I can call him and see if we can crash there while we figure everything out."

I held up my hand. "Give me a second to figure out

where this Connor lives before doing that. Canada's a pretty huge place." Once I had his address typed in, I waited for the map to come up; his house was five hours away. "All right, it takes a few hours to get there. He lives in Kingston. If we leave now we can get there late morning."

"Really? That's where my friend lives too."

"He your best friend?"

Nodding, he scrolled through his phone until he found some pictures of Hadley with both of them. "He and Hadley were good friends. He wouldn't tell anyone what we were doing," Nick said, showing me the pictures.

"What's his last name?" I asked.

His brows furrowed. "Doherty, why?"

"How long have you known him?"

He closed his eyes, pursing his lips. "About two years."

I skimmed through Connor's file again and clicked on the others associated with him. There were about twenty men. MacCarthy, no. Carroll, no. Shit, where did I see it? Then I found it.

"Give me your phone," I ordered. I held the picture up beside the photo on file. They looked exactly alike, only one was much older than the other.

Stunned, Nick gasped. "Holy shit."

CHAPTER 31

HADLEY

My head pounded. At least there wasn't any light coming through the window to make it worse. I cracked an eye open and groaned; it was dark outside. For a moment, I almost forgot where I was, but then one name was all it took to drag me back.

"Blake," I whispered frantically. Jumping out of my bed, I scrambled into the closet and pulled a handful of clothes down. I took off my shirt and shorts and pulled new ones on. Adrenaline coursed through my veins. Rushing to the window, I lifted it up and felt the cool breeze brush across my skin. I half expected an alarm to go off, but luckily, it didn't.

Taking a deep breath, I lifted one leg over and

straddled the sill. The drop down could easily break bones if I landed wrong. "Here I go."

"I wouldn't do that if I were you," a voice called. Hands grabbed me and pulled me in. I fell to the floor and Connor towered over me, shutting the window. "Now what exactly do you think you're doing?"

I jumped to my feet and pushed against his chest. "Where's Blake? If you so much as touched him, I'll kill you myself." I pushed him again. "Where is he?"

Grabbing me around the waist, he pulled me into his body and slammed a hand over my mouth. I tried to fight him off, but we fell onto the bed, him pinning me with his weight. "Stop fighting me, Hadley. Blake is fine. I called and warned him about the attack hours ago."

Eyes burning, I sagged in his arms. He was alive. "Why are you doing this?" I said into his hand.

"I'm not the one doing anything. I want to help you, but you have to work with me. I'll let you go now, if you promise not to fight me. Deal?" I nodded and he slowly uncovered my mouth. "Good. I'm getting off you now." Once he moved away, I scrambled to the other side of the bed and onto the floor.

"Why am I here?" It was still dark, but I could see him move across the room to the sitting chair.

He sat down and sighed. "You're not going to like my answer."

"I don't care. Anything is better than not knowing."

He ran his hands over his face and then clasped them in his lap. "You're here because everyone back home thinks you're dead."

"Excuse me? Wait, you're kidding, right?" It had to be a joke. Maybe I was a victim of one of those prank TV shows that like to mess with celebrities.

From across the darkened room, I could see his serious gaze. There would be no TV crews busting in to say it was a joke. In that moment, all of my hopes and dreams shattered. "Oh my God, you're not."

He shook his head. "We orchestrated your death to make it look like an accident. For the past couple of years, your father had been getting threats on your life. I guess you can say he got tired of it and wanted to take matters into his own hands. That's why he asked us to do this for him."

I felt sick and betrayed. How could my father take my life away like that? "Who is *us*?" I demanded. "Are you with the government?"

"No. I'm involved in something much worse."

Swallowing hard, I stepped back. "Like what, the mafia?" When all he did was stare at me, I had my answer. "How did my father get involved with you?"

"He was looking for someone qualified to be your bodyguard."

I crossed my arms over my chest and snorted.

"Of course, you're qualified. I bet you kill people for a living." A small smile splayed across his lips and it infuriated me. "It's not funny," I snapped.

"Hadley, you have no clue what I do."

"That might be a good thing. I'd hate to end up at the bottom of the lake with cement boots."

Chuckling, he checked his watch and stood. "That's just bullshit you see on TV." He started for the door, but I stepped in his way.

"Who was the other guy you were talking to last night?"

His smile faded. "You'll find out tomorrow. If I tell you now, it'll ruin my plan."

"So, I'm supposed to just trust you?"

"I'm the only one here you can. Now what I need you to do is play along with everything he says. We don't have much time."

"Why is that?" I asked, heart racing.

The muscles in his jaw tensed. "In two days, you'll be leaving for Ireland. Once you go over there, you won't be coming back. He'll never let you go."

Terror racked through my body. "What does he want with me?"

"You, Hadley. He's wanted you for a long time now. I just didn't realize how far his obsession had gone. That's why he wanted Blake out of the way. He used your father to get to you. It was his plan all along."

"And you're sure Blake's okay?"

He nodded. "Dillon never called to confirm the kill. My guess is Blake got to him first."

"Thank God." Breathing a sigh of relief, I sagged against the wall. "What am I going to do? How can I look at my father after this?"

"He did it to protect you, Hadley. He just went about it the wrong way. I told him I could help him, and that's when all of this came into play. He never thought about what it would do to you or your career. All he wanted was to keep you safe . . . alive."

"It's your fault then?"

He shrugged. "Not entirely. But soon, you'll be home and all of this will be over."

"Will it? I guess I'll have to see it to believe it. Does Blake think I'm dead too?"

"Yes, but he's a smart man. By now, he's probably figured out you're alive. He'll come for you."

My gut clenched. "What if he doesn't?"

"He will. I'll make sure of it." Opening the door, he peered down both sides of the hall.

"Why are you helping me?"

He glanced back at me, his gaze full of pain. Lifting his hand, he circled a strand of my hair through his fingers. "You remind me of someone."

"Who?"

His gaze darkened and he shook his head. "Forget it.

Let's just say I have my reasons. Now go back to bed."
He disappeared down the hall and I just stood there,
wide awake. There was no sleep to be had.

For the rest of the night, I sat at the window and
watched the sun come up. How could a place so
beautiful, be filled with so much evil?

"Knock, knock," Connor announced, knocking on
my door.

"Come in." I watched him walk in through the
reflection in the window.

"I'm here to escort you to lunch."

"Like I could eat right now," I grumbled, turning to
face him.

His body tensed. "You have to, Hadley. You're not
supposed to know anything."

"Don't worry, I can do this. Will *he* be eating with
me?"

He nodded. "That's the whole point. And whatever
you do, don't mention Blake, or your friends, or
anything about using a fucking phone. Just spend time
with him and get through the day. He's not the same
guy you think you know."

My hands started to shake. *I can do this.*

Opening the door, he held it wide for me. "Let's go."

Taking a deep breath, I walked past him into the hall. He stayed by my side and whispered encouraging words, but all I could hear was the pounding of my heart. We stopped at a set of double doors and he nodded encouragingly before opening them up. At the far end of the table sat two place settings, both with covered dishes.

Connor nudged me forward. "Take a seat. He'll be in here in a minute."

"Aren't you staying with me?"

Shaking his head, he retreated to the door. "He wants to be alone with you."

Once he shut the door behind him, I sucked in a breath and held it, as I made my way to the table. The sound of footsteps sounded on the marble floor just outside of the room and when the door opened, I froze.

"Miss Rivers, would you like something to drink?" a soft voice asked.

I blew out my held breath and grabbed my chest. The lady was petite, probably in her mid-forties, with dark brown hair, and dressed in a typical blue and white maid's uniform.

"Hi." I was at a loss for words. It was the first time I'd seen someone in the house other than scary mobster men.

"Would you care for a glass of wine, water, or soda?"

"May I have a bottle of water?" That way I could tell

if someone had spiked it.

She bowed her head and smiled. "I'll be right back."

It didn't take her long to get my bottle and when I opened it, the lid was still attached. I guzzled it down and almost had the whole bottle gone when I heard his voice.

"Calm down, killer."

When I saw his face, I gasped and choked on the water.

He rushed over and patted my back as I coughed it out. "You okay?" he asked, kneeling down beside me. He smiled and my heart broke. Connor had to have been wrong. There was no way Tristan would hurt me. Plus, he didn't have an Irish accent like the guy from last night.

"Tristan, what are you doing here?"

He sat down at the head of the table and grabbed my hand. "I came to see you. After everything you've been through, your father thought it'd be good for you to see a familiar face. Plus, he felt it'd be a great idea for you to go on a vacation. I have family in Ireland and told him I could take you there."

I forced a smile. "Ireland? Wow, that's really sweet of you, but I should probably be getting back to work. My producer is dying to get me back in the studio."

The door to the room opened and the maid brought in another bottle of water and a glass of wine for Tristan.

She set my bottle of water down in front of me and lifted the lid that covered my plate. "*Bain sult as*," she said sweetly.

I stared at her like she'd lost her mind.

Tristan laughed. "She said enjoy. It's Irish."

Act normal. Picking up my fork, I stabbed a piece of broccoli and put it in my mouth. "I didn't know you knew how to speak Irish."

She lifted the lid over his food and retreated from the room. "I know how to speak seven different languages. It'll come in handy when I take you overseas. There's so much to see and do over there. You probably won't want to come back."

"It sounds amazing. Too bad I can't stay over there forever," I laughed. The more he talked about Ireland, the more I started to believe he *was* the one. For the entire time I'd known him, he'd never mentioned anything about Ireland, other than the times he spent there in college.

"Do you want to go for a walk after lunch?" he asked.

I finished my food and guzzled down the second bottle of water. "Sure, if we can. The men here don't like to let me walk around freely. It's like a prison. I guess they're afraid I'm going to run away or something."

"Why would you want to do that? This place is amazing."

I shrugged, pretending to be baffled. "I don't know. Maybe they think the media will try to get in somehow. You know how they like to follow me."

"That's probably it," he agreed. "They're just being protective of you." What a load of bullshit. They were being protective all right, but it wasn't for my safety. "Ready to go for a walk? I saw the gardens when I pulled in. I know how you like stuff like that."

"Sure, let's go."

He pulled out my chair and opened the back set of doors that led down a long hallway. Gesturing for me to go first, he followed closely behind, putting his hand on my lower back.

"I hadn't seen this part of the house. How do you know where to go?" I asked, gauging his reaction.

"Just a guess," he said.

Did he really think I was that naïve? Obviously, he'd underestimated me. Once we got outside, I could breathe easier. I half expected one of his suited men to follow us around, but there was no one in sight.

"How are you holding up after the whole Nick thing? He took it pretty hard when you called it off."

To avoid his stare, I bent down to smell one of the wild roses. "I know, but it was all pretend. I never wanted him to fall for me. We only did it to ward off the stalker."

"Yeah, I know. Who do you think came up with the

idea?"

Furrowing my brows, I glanced up at him. "He did, didn't he?"

Tristan snorted. "Nah, I did. I was going to confront you about it and see if you wanted me to help you out. But . . . he did it first."

"Oh wow, he never told me," I replied, getting to my feet. Was that what Tristan wanted me to believe, or was it the truth? If the roles were switched, it made me wonder where I'd be now.

His gaze darkened. "Why would he, when he had you right where he wanted you?"

"Why didn't you tell me it was your idea?"

He shrugged. "Would you have chosen me instead? You almost kissed me that night. I remember it, even if you don't."

Back then, I *was* attracted to him and I probably would've picked him over Nick. Now, I was thankful Nick approached me first. "That was a long time ago, Tristan. And it's not like the plan worked anyway. Dane still killed Scott and shot Nick. If it was you in his place, you could've been hurt."

"I'm not like Nick, Hadley. No one would've gotten past me. I could've protected you." His phone rang and he pulled it out of his pocket, eyes narrowing when he focused on the screen. "I have to take this. Are you okay out here?"

"Yeah, I'm fine," I said, waving my hands. "Go."

Turning on his heel, he rushed inside and answered the call. It made me wonder who it was.

I stayed outside for another few minutes before retreating indoors. Everything was quiet. There were a few sounds coming from the kitchen when I walked past, but it was probably Ingrid. I strolled past another room and then stopped when I realized it was a fully stocked library with floor to ceiling bookcases. It was breathtaking.

Sneaking inside, I skimmed over the bookcases in awe, grabbing one of my all-time favorite classics, *Pride and Prejudice.* Walking into the sitting room connected to the library, I sat by the window and opened the book. If I couldn't literally escape, I would find an outlet somewhere else. I cracked the book open and froze when that familiar Irish voice growled from behind a closed door. There was no mistaking who the voice belonged to anymore.

Sliding out of my seat, I tiptoed to the door that connected to another room.

"Why the fuck is he coming today?" he argued.

Another guy answered, but I didn't recognize his voice. It wasn't Connor and it wasn't Shades. "He said he wants to spend time with Hadley before she leaves for Ireland."

"*Cad a pian goddamn an asal,*" Tristan replied angrily.

What the hell does that mean?

"What do you want to do about it?"

Tristan huffed. "You know what to do. Make it look like a suicide. With Hadley's death, it'll be believable."

Clasping a hand over my mouth, I held in my cries and backed away slowly. I had to find Connor so he could warn my dad. When I turned to make a run for it, I shrieked as an arm grabbed me around the waist. "What are you doing? Let me go," I shouted.

It was Shades.

The door to the room opened and Tristan walked out, followed by the other person he had told to kill my dad. His eyes were cold and detached, very unnerving. Tristan looked at me and then at Shades. "What the fuck's going on?"

Anger boiled in my veins. How could the playful, easy-going Tristan I'd known for the past two years be such a murderous bastard? Gaze narrowed, he stepped toward me and looked into my eyes.

"I saw her sneaking out of the sitting room," Shades reported. I tried to jerk out of his hold, but he gripped me harder.

Tristan studied me and I refused to back down. The time for playing along was gone. "You know, don't you?" he asked, speaking with his Irish accent.

How could he have fooled us for so long?

I lifted my chin defiantly. "I know you're a lying son

of a bitch. If you hurt my father, I'll kill you myself."

A wide grin spread across his face. He didn't even look like Tristan anymore. "It looks like you and Connor are closer than I thought. I don't like it." He beckoned the other guy forward with a wave of his hand. "Find Connor and make sure he doesn't come back."

"Tristan, no!" I cried, jerking my arm away from Shades. He grabbed me around the waist and slammed a hand over my mouth.

The other guy grabbed Tristan's shoulder. "Sir, he's your uncle. Your father is the only one who makes those decisions. I can't condone it."

Tristan's eyes blazed. "Do you see my father here?" he growled through clenched teeth. "This is *my* territory and what I say goes. Now do as I say, or you'll be next."

Nodding, the other guy marched off and disappeared from the room.

"What should we do with her?" Shades asked. I elbowed him in the ribs and he grunted.

Tristan glared at him and then at me. "Take her to my room. I'll deal with her personally."

Shades lifted me in his arms, one hand still over my mouth and the other wrapped excruciatingly tight across my chest. I struggled to breathe, as everything was too constricting. He carried me up the stairs to the third floor, and by then I felt like I was going to pass out.

As soon as we got to Tristan's room, he dropped me

to the floor and I gasped for air. "You're lucky you're his," he hissed low, glaring at me with soulless blue eyes.

I jumped to my feet. "Or what?"

He stepped closer and snarled. "Or I'd beat the shit out of you for hitting me. Where we come from, lassies like you respect their men. You'll learn soon enough." Turning on his heel, he stormed out of the room and slammed the door.

I didn't even have to try the knob to know he'd locked me in. Heart pounding, I rushed to the windows and peered out. I had no clue how to save my dad or Connor. Hell, I didn't even know how to save myself.

CHAPTER 32

HADLEY

"Are you calmed down yet?" Tristan asked as he entered his room.

Fighting him was no use. I'd either find myself drugged or beaten, and there was no way I could help my father in that state. "Go to hell. I don't even know who you are anymore."

Grabbing my arm, he turned me around and pulled me to him. I used to love looking at his hazel eyes, but now they made me sick. "There are some things you need to know before I take you to Ireland. One, you're mine. Listen to me and do as I say, and I will give you everything you'd ever want. You'll learn to love me."

I scoffed. "You expect me to love you after taking

everything away from me? Have you lost your mind?"

"Let's get something straight, love. Your *father* took everything away from you. It was his decision to fake your death."

"Yeah, after Connor coerced him into it," I snapped. "It was *you* who wanted me to disappear."

He trailed a finger down my chin and I stiffened. "When I want something, I get it. This was the only way I could get you all to myself. No more Blake, no more Nick, no more sharing you with the world. Just you and me."

Eyes wide, I backed out of his touch. Why hadn't I seen it sooner? "Out of the way? It was you, wasn't it? You're the one who killed Scott and shot Nick."

His lips spread wide. "You're a smart girl. He deserved it too, taking my idea to be with you . . ." He kissed his teeth in annoyance. "It all worked out perfectly when that crackhead took the fall. The idiot was probably scared the police were going to bust him for the drugs and went on the run. It was all the ammunition I needed for your father. Once your bodyguard was gone, Connor was right there. Just a few more death threats on your life and the deal was sealed." He stepped forward and backed me into the wall, blocking me in with his arms and hips.

"It was you the entire time," I stated.

"From the very beginning, love. For two years, I've

been trying to get you, and now you're here. Tomorrow we leave for Ireland. Your future and everyone else's depends on you."

"What are you saying?"

Pressing his body against mine, I could feel his erection against my hip and thought I might vomit. Trailing his nose up my neck, he breathed me in. "Am I correct in assuming you want your father alive?" he asked, murmuring the words in my ear.

My eyes burned. "Yes."

He trailed a hand over my breast and rested it on my hips. "I can promise to keep him alive, but you have to show me how bad you want it." He closed his lips over mine and I jerked away.

"Why are you forcing me to do this?"

Grasping my chin, he pulled me back. "I don't want to force you, love. If I have to, I will. But I want you to enjoy this as much as I do. All you have to do is give me a chance and I'll make sure everyone you love and care about stays safe. Defy me and you'll see how ruthless I can get. Now," he said, murmuring against my lips, "kiss me like you mean it."

Tears spilled over my cheeks and I closed my eyes. Opening my lips, I let him kiss me. It made me sick to feel his tongue against mine, his hands all over my body.

Moaning, he pulled back. "Now that's what I'm talking about. You just gave your father and extra day to live." He kissed me again and sucked my bottom lip. "When I come back, we can work on giving him another week." He cupped his hand between my legs. "Be ready for me."

I held my breath and waited for him to leave before breaking down. As soon as the door shut, I fell to my knees. I knew what he wanted, but I didn't know if I had the strength to do it; especially if I had to do it every day. I'd rather be dead.

CHAPTER 33

BLAKE

"For the longest time, I never understood why he felt the need to have that much security," Nick said. "Now I know." He passed me the binoculars and I scanned the grounds. There was only one person patrolling, but that didn't mean there weren't more.

"Where do you think he would keep her?"

He shook his head. "Not sure exactly. But it'd either be on the second or third floor. That's where all of the bedrooms are. Downstairs you have the kitchen, library, and other entertainment rooms."

"Did he ever have security walking around?"

"Nah, not ever. This is a first."

Probably because he had precious cargo in the

house. The sound of a car caught my ear. "Someone's coming." A small, red sports car came barreling down the road and I recognized it immediately.

"It's Hadley's father," Nick pointed out.

"I know." I held up the binoculars and watched him get through the gate with no issues. "Well, this just got interesting."

"Do you think he put the hit out on you?"

My blood boiled. "I don't know. If he did, he'll fucking regret it." George got out of the car and walked right into the house.

"She'll be fine, right?" Nick asked.

"I fucking hope so. Whatever happens tonight, I need you to be all in. There's no hesitating. If you want her out alive, you have to be willing to do whatever's necessary."

He nodded. "I won't hesitate, even if I have to kill Tristan myself."

"Even knowing you might get killed in the process? If you want to back out, now's the time to do it. I can do this myself." The last thing I needed was to worry about him while we were in there. I saw how upset Hadley was when he was in the hospital, and I didn't want her having to go through that again.

Nick huffed. "I'll be fine. I'm a fucking hockey player. I like to kick ass."

Rolling my eyes, I glanced down at my watch. We

had two more hours for the sun to go down. We'd already been out there for over three, and it felt like a fucking eternity. Usually, I'd go in guns blazing, but I couldn't do that, not with Hadley's life on the line. My phone vibrated in my pocket and I pulled it out. It showed up as Hadley.

Nick glanced down at it. "Why does he keep calling from her phone?"

"Because he knows I'll answer it." I accepted the call and growled low into the phone. "What?"

"I see you're still alive. I knew you would be."

"Can't say the same for you. What do you want?"

"We're on the same side, Mr. Evans. And right now, Hadley needs our help. I need you here, *tonight*. We don't have much time."

I scoffed. "Don't worry, I already know where you are. I don't need your help." I hung up, not waiting for a reply. I didn't trust him, not when he was one of the reasons Hadley was gone.

Nick stared at me. "What?" I snapped.

"It sounds like he's really trying to help."

"Doesn't matter. I can't trust anyone but myself. I learned that the hard way."

"I know what you mean."

For the next couple of hours, I showed Nick how to hold his pistol and how to load it. One of Mason's guys had given us extra ammo, since I only had enough for myself. Nick needed to be prepared. The guy might be a pain in my ass, but I could see it in his eyes, he wasn't afraid. It was what I needed.

The sky began to turn dark, and it was time to move. Once everything was packed up, we moved closer to the house so I could set up. Nick pointed to the house. "How are we going to get in?"

I opened my laptop and typed away. "I'm going to override the security system. For just a few brief minutes, we'll be able to climb the fence undetected. As soon as we get in, I want to find Hadley and then get you two out of there."

"What about you?" he stormed, jerking his head toward me.

"I'm not leaving until they pay for what they did."

"Hadley's not going to like that."

I knew she wouldn't, but she had no choice. "She'll just have to understand."

A twig snapped behind us a couple hundred feet back. I tensed and so did Nick. "What was that?" he whispered.

"Someone's here." I pointed to one of the large trees beside us. "Crouch low in front of that tree. We don't want to shoot out here."

"Don't shoot, got it." He crawled over to the tree and crouched low.

It was so dark, I could barely see him, but I had a

night sensor on my pistol that helped. Another twig snapped and when I pointed my gun in the general direction, I found what I was looking for. It was Connor. As quietly as I could, I stood and took small, calculated steps through the brush. Without him knowing, I circled around and came up behind him.

"I told you I didn't need you," I warned.

He lifted his hands and held them out. "I told Hadley you would come."

"Where is she?"

"Either in her room or Tristan's. I saw them taking her away, kicking and screaming. She obviously found out something while I was gone. The next thing I knew, they were coming to my house to put a bullet in my head."

"And why would they do that?"

He sighed. "Because Tristan and I don't see eye to eye. When I found out what he was up to, I challenged him on it. And if there's one thing you don't do, it's cross him."

"Why did you then?"

His shoulders stiffened. "You're not the only one he took something from."

"You expect me to believe this?"

"No, but it's all you got. He's planning to take her to Ireland tomorrow and as soon as she's with our people, getting her out will be nearly impossible."

"What does her father have to do with this? Did he order the hit on me?"

He shook his head. "No, he's clueless. That was all Tristan. George doesn't even know he was the one involved here. Every message was passed through me. The man was desperate after the last threat, so he asked me to fake her death. Obviously, he doesn't know the consequences of dealing with my kind."

Nick left his spot by the tree and stormed over. "Why does Tristan want to take Hadley?"

If Connor was surprised at his presence, he didn't show it. "Because he's obsessed with her; has been for years. Can I drop my arms now?"

Lowering my gun, I stepped around him and he dropped his arms. "Are you trying to say he's been here this whole time just for her?"

"As fucked up as it sounds, that's exactly what I'm saying. He orchestrated this whole thing, studying her and her friends." He turned to Nick. "Including you. He hated you with Hadley. Thinks you tried to take her away from him."

Nick tensed. "What a fucking bastard. It wouldn't surprise me if he was the one who broke into Hadley's that night and killed Scott."

"And shot you," I added.

Connor glanced back and forth at us. "I've thought about that. He denied it when I asked him. He claims he was with a girl that night. If I went snooping, he'd know." He shrugged and pointed at the house. "But now we have a bigger problem. Tristan's plan was to take Hadley away before her father got back. I don't know what the fuck he's doing here early. Tristan isn't going to like that. My guess is, they'll kill him to keep him out of the way. Tristan gets off on getting rid of *obstacles*."

The sky grew darker and time was running out. "All right, let's get this shit started," I said, hurrying to my laptop. "How many people does he have in there?"

"Just two. I'm assuming Dillon is missing because you got rid of him already?"

Nick snorted. "He's not dead, but Evans fucked him up."

They talked back and forth while I typed away and got everything ready to go. All I had to do was click one button and the system would be down. "Where should we go in at?" I asked.

Connor cleared his throat. "The window in Hadley's room is unlocked. I caught her trying to escape last night. When I shut it, I never locked it."

"Why did she try to leave?"

"Tristan drugged her and thought she was passed out when he said he wanted you dead. When she woke up, she tried to get to you. I was there to stop her."

Clenching my teeth, I clicked the override button.

There was no telling what all that fucker had done to her. "This ends tonight. Let's go."

We took off for the fence and got over it with ease. Without the override, we wouldn't have been able to withstand the electrical current running through the wires. It'd be like getting struck by lightning. Once again, I was thankful for my many connections.

When we got to the back of the house, I climbed up the side and opened the window Connor pointed to. Hadley wasn't in there, but I slid in and helped Nick and Connor inside.

"She must be in Tristan's room," Connor hissed.

The thought made me so goddamn pissed I couldn't see straight. I stormed for the door. "I'm going up there to find her."

Nick pulled out his gun and had it ready. "And I'll try to find her father. The faster we find them both, the quicker we can get the hell out of here."

I didn't like him going out on his own, but he knew the risks. "What are you going to do?" I asked Connor.

Eyes blazing, he held up his gun. "I'm ready for my own revenge."

They both took off down the stairs and I went up to the third floor. The hallway was dark but I knew exactly where to go when a figure caught my eye. Tristan had one of his goons stationed right outside of a room. Unfortunately, I couldn't shoot or it'd alert the whole house. Sneaking into one of the other rooms, I closed the door and lightly scraped my fingers across it.

"Come on, bastard," I grumbled.

The sound of his footsteps steadily approached and the door creaked open. As soon as I saw the gun in his hand, I grabbed his wrist and twisted. He started to shout, but I wrapped my other arm around his face and snapped his neck. One down, two to go. I pulled him further into the room and stole the keys off his belt.

Hurrying down the hall, I studied the lock. There were a ton of keys, but only a couple of brass ones; that was what I needed. I tried the first, second, and third one, but they didn't work. I got down to the last one and it turned home. Taking a deep breath, I turned the knob and opened the door, not knowing what the hell I was going to see.

CHAPTER 34

HADLEY

For the past couple of hours, I dreaded the moment Tristan would walk through that door and now the time had finally come. My eyes burned, but I refused to let him break me. No matter what happened, I was going to stand strong with my head held high. Could I fight him off? Maybe, but not for long. I knew I didn't stand a chance in the long run, at least not alone. My father was there somewhere, and I didn't know if Tristan was going to keep his word. I had no doubt he would kill him if I defied him.

Closing my eyes, I clutched my stomach and took a deep breath. I felt sick and disgusted with myself for what I was about to do. There was no choice as long as my dad's life was on the line. Maybe I could make myself sick and puke on him when he tried to fuck me. Either way, I had to figure it out. The door opened and closed, his footsteps drawing closer. My heart pounded harder with each passing second. He knew I'd do anything to keep my family and friends safe. How could I lay there and pretend to enjoy him fucking me?

"Please, Tristan," I begged, "don't make me do this." Holding my stomach tighter, I fought the urge to vomit. I might need it later.

"Hadley." Gasping, I opened my eyes and froze. "Hadley, are you okay?"

Slowly, I turned around, tears falling the moment I saw him. He approached slowly, staring at me as if I would break. Little did he know, he gave me all the strength I needed. "You're here!" I cried, rushing into his arms.

His arms closed in around me and he held me so tight I could barely breathe, but I didn't care. He was there. That was all that mattered. "I'm here," he murmured. I didn't want to let him go, but he pulled back and clutched my face in his firm grip, his gray eyes dark and dangerous. "What did he do to you?"

"Nothing," I said, hoping he couldn't see the lie in my face. His gaze narrowed and I looked away; he could see right through me. "Other than drugging me, he hasn't had the chance to do much. But my father's here somewhere and he's in trouble. So is Connor."

Grabbing my hand, he pulled me to the door. "Connor's fine. He's here with me and Nick."

"Nick?" I hissed. "Why is he here?"

He stopped in front of the door and sighed. "He cares about you, Hadley. As much as I dislike the guy, he's actually been quite useful. Now let's go." We snuck out into the hall, and he froze, pulling out his phone.

"Who is it?" I whispered.

"It's Nick. He's downstairs with your father. He needs help getting him out."

Breathing a sigh of relief, I followed him down the stairs. My father was still alive. "Where's Tristan? He has two other guys with him," I informed him.

Squeezing my hand, he jerked me into a darkened corner, his gaze on a security camera by the ceiling. "There's only one now."

"What happened to the other one?" I asked.

He glanced at me quickly and then averted his gaze back to the camera. "He's dead. There was no other way." Once the camera turned toward the other side of the room, we took off down the hall. "Nick said it's the second door on the right." We got to the door and he guided me out of the way. "Let me go in there first. It might be a trap." Holding his gun in one hand, he turned the knob with the other. The room was half lit and the only thing I could see over Blake's shoulder was

Nick's head. Blake glanced back at me. "We're good, come on."

We rushed inside to find Nick trying to get my father free from his restraints. His head lolled to the side and he was bound to a chair, clearly drugged.

"Dad," I gasped, racing over to him. I tried to lift his head, but he was out.

Nick passed Blake the knife, then lifted me up in his arms. "Thank fucking God you're okay. We thought you were dead."

"I would've been if you two didn't show up. There is no way I could've submitted to his wishes." I shivered at the thought.

He set me down and went straight back to helping Blake. Once my father was free, Nick hauled him up by one side and I took the other. Blake peered out the door and motioned for us to follow him. We got to the main foyer and all I could see was the front door beckoning us closer. Almost there.

Blake grasped my chin and kissed me. "I want you to go with Nick and hide in the woods. I'll be out there soon." I started to protest, but he kissed me again. "Don't, Hadley. Just do as I say."

I didn't want him leaving me, not when I just got him back.

"Hads, let's go," Nick urged. We started for the door, but it slammed open and we stopped dead in our tracks.

Nick pulled out his gun, but we were in a standoff, and the other guy was most likely faster.

"Going somewhere?" Shades taunted, pointing his gun straight at Nick's face.

Blake's gun clicked from behind. "Drop it."

"Maybe you should drop yours," Tristan called out as he entered the room.

Shades smirked and walked around the edge of the room, while Nick followed his movements. Now we were facing Tristan and Blake, but Tristan was behind Blake who in turn had his gun still pointed at Shades. Tristan was in the clear.

"You lying sack of shit," Nick spat. "How could you do this?"

Tristan rolled his eyes. "Pretty easy, actually. My only mistake was not killing you."

Nick tensed. "So it *was* you."

"Nothing personal, brother. You had something I wanted and I used you to get to it. Speaking of which," he noted, turning his dark eyes to me, "you're not in my bed where you're supposed to be. I told you bad things would happen if you disobeyed me."

"Tristan, please," I begged. "You don't have to do this. I'll go with you." Blake shook his head, but I had no choice. I couldn't gamble with their lives. Taking a deep breath, I let go of my father and glanced at Nick. "I'm sorry." One step at a time, I walked over to Tristan and stood by his side.

"Good girl. Now let's make sure you don't do it again." Then everything moved in slow motion as he pointed his gun at my father and fired.

"No!" I screamed, falling to the floor.

My father hissed, but was still out of it from the drugs. Nick grunted with holding his weight and eventually dropped him to the floor so he could keep his gun trained on Shades. Blood oozed onto the floor from his thigh and all I could see was red.

"Bastard," I shouted, glaring straight at Tristan.

"It was just a knick, love. A simple reminder to take my threats seriously." He edged closer to Blake. "Now what am I going to do about this one? That is, if I'm correct in assuming this is the infamous Blake Evans. I heard you killed one of my guys. Not an easy task."

"Two," Blake pointed out. "The other one's upstairs." Tristan growled and slammed the heel of his gun down on the back of Blake's head. Hissing, he fell to his knees, a trail of blood dripping down his neck.

I choked in terror. "Tristan, stop! I'll go with you if you just leave them alone. I'll do whatever you want." It was a lie, but I had to get him away from Blake.

Turning his attention to me, he smirked. "So you'll let me fuck you whenever I want?"

By the look in his eyes, he'd kill them all no matter what I did. I just needed to give them more time.

Clenching my teeth, I closed my eyes and nodded.

"I can't hear you, Hadley," Tristan taunted.

My eyes snapped open and I shot to my feet. "Yes!" Adrenaline coursed through my veins. "You want me now? Let's go." He stared at me like I'd lost my mind, and maybe I had. All I knew was, I had to do something. Pulse racing, I stalked past him toward the stairs, not knowing what the hell I was going to do.

An idea hit me and I had a split second to act. Grabbing the antique Celtic cross Tristan had showcased on one of his tables, I turned and hurled it at his head. He saw it in enough time to duck, but it gave Blake the time he needed to act.

Then everything moved in super speed all around me. Blake and Tristan battled it out while Nick and Shades fought on the other side of the room. I didn't know who to help or where to go. A gun fired and I screamed, but then I was dragged out of the room from behind and let go.

Breathing hard, Connor pulled out his phone and handed it to me. "Take this. I've already called for help, but it'll take them a while to get here. Right now, you need to get out of here." Another gunshot fired and he pushed me toward the back door. "Go, now!" He charged off into the fight, but I couldn't leave them. Instead, I went right back into the line of fire.

There was blood everywhere, yet no one was down.

Nick had blood soaking the left side of his shirt and I could see his energy waning. He backed into the wall and gripped his arm. "Nick!" I raced toward him and helped him over to my dad. "What happened?"

He grimaced in pain. "The fucker shot me in the shoulder. I think this is a clear sign that I need to stick to hockey."

"Are you okay? Where did he go?"

"I'm fine. I think he took off to find you. I need to warn Connor." He started to get up and I squeezed his arm. Connor could handle Shades.

"No, you need to help me get my dad out of here. I can't do it by myself." Nodding, he helped lift my dad to his feet. We carried him outside and all the way down the driveway. Nick pressed the button for the gate and it opened. "Where are we going?"

He nodded toward the woods. "There's a spot up ahead with all of our supplies."

As soon as we got there, I pulled out one of Blake's shirts from his bag and ripped it in half. I wrapped one around my dad's leg and the other around Nick's shoulder. Something else caught my eye and I picked it up.

"That's not a toy, Hadley," Nick warned.

"I know," I agreed, holding the gun in my hands. Turning on my heel, I marched straight back toward the house.

"Hadley, no! Stop!"

I couldn't stop. There was no time.

CHAPTER 35

HADLEY

More gunshots fired and I ran as fast as I could. Shades could be seen through the window, getting to his feet but I couldn't see Connor. Where was he? Shades hobbled across the floor, gun drawn. *No!* I raced up the stairs and pointed my gun at his chest. Blake was on top of Tristan, his fists hitting flesh, he didn't see Shades coming.

I pulled the trigger and the next thing I knew, he was on the floor, bleeding out from a wound in his gut. Not where I was aiming, but at least I hit my mark. He grunted in pain and reached for his gun. Another shot rang out and I screamed, turning my head away from the bloody carnage.

Gun drawn, Connor stood by my side, his expression full of turmoil. "It's over, Tristan," he growled low.

Blake slammed Tristan's head on the marble floor and stood. He was covered in blood and the whole right side of his face was bruised. Breathing hard, he cocked his gun and pointed it at Tristan, who he allowed to get unsteadily to his feet.

Even faced with death, Tristan glared defiantly at us. Blake put his finger on the trigger and his muscles twitched. He was about to pull.

"Blake, no," I warned.

Furrowing his brows, he glanced at me. "There's no choice here, Hadley. This has to end. He has to pay for what he did to you."

Connor spoke up. "Don't worry about it, I'll take care of him."

Tristan swayed on his feet. "You gonna kill me, uncle?"

Connor winced and pointed the gun straight at his head. "You have no idea how long I've waited for this."

Tristan scoffed. "Is this about that whore of yours?"

"She wasn't a *whore*." His voice boomed throughout the room and I trembled. I'd never seen him so angry; it was frightening. "Alannah was mine and you killed her! You raped her and when you found out she was pregnant, you made it look like a suicide. It wasn't even your fucking child; it was mine!" He pulled out a piece of paper from the back of his pocket and threw it at Tristan. "She told me everything you did, you son of a bitch. She knew you were going to kill her."

Clapping a hand over my mouth, I gasped in horror.

Blake lowered his gun and put an arm around me. "Turn around and keep walking," he murmured, pulling me back. "It's between them now."

It was hard for him to walk away, but Connor needed the revenge more than he did. I was the one still alive, Alannah wasn't. Turning my back, Tristan growled and started to shout, but I couldn't hear what he said. A gunshot fired and I heard his body hit the floor with a loud thunk.

As soon as we got out of the house, I jumped into Blake's arms. "I love you so much," I cried.

He breathed me in, holding me tight. "I love you too, princess."

Tears welled in my eyes and I laughed. I'd missed hearing him call me that. "How did you know I wasn't dead?"

Brushing the hair off my face, he slid his fingers down and cupped my cheek. "I didn't at first. I thought you were dead. It fucked me up more than anything. But then things didn't add up and I couldn't live with that. I had to have proof you were gone, and how it truly happened. That's why I went to Burnsville and had Logan help me."

"Logan?" I asked, wide-eyed.

He smiled. "He's the one who got the satellite video for me. It showed the crash and then Connor getting you out of the car. After that, I knew what to do."

"What if you were too late? What if Tristan had taken me to Ireland?"

His gaze grew dark. "I would've gone over there and fought for you. Nothing was going to keep me away."

Over his shoulder, I watched Connor exit the house. I couldn't imagine what it felt like to have to be around Tristan after what he'd done to him. It was vile and completely heartbreaking.

"Connor," I called. He walked over and I threw my arms around his neck. "Thank you."

It took him a few seconds, but he returned the embrace and let me go. By the pain in his eyes, I could tell killing Tristan took a lot out of him. Tristan was his nephew, his family. "You're welcome. Sooner or later, he would've killed you too. If not physically, emotionally. I wasn't about to let him do that to another innocent girl."

"I'm sorry about Alannah."

He averted his gaze. "Killing Tristan won't bring her back, but it had to be done."

I glanced at them both. "What happens now?"

Blake put his arm around me. "We wait for the police to come, answer their questions, and go home. Then you get the jollies of dodging the press." That was going to be a nightmare. I'd been in the news more in the past two months than I had in my whole career. It was going to explode when word got out that I was alive.

"What about you?" I asked Connor.

His gaze landed on Blake and he was the one who answered. "His people will probably have him sent back to Ireland, where they can dish out punishment. Am I right?"

Connor nodded. "Killing him will be the ultimate sin in my brother's eyes, no matter what he did to deserve it."

Sirens blared in the distance; the police were coming. "What if you're dead?" I asked.

"We could say one of Tristan's guys killed you and buried you somewhere. That could work, right?" I glanced up at Blake, hoping he'd agree.

He squeezed my shoulder. "I think you've been hanging around these guys a little too long."

"Not a bad idea," Connor added. "But I'd need your full cooperation. You'd have to lie for me."

The sirens were getting closer. "We'll do it, now go," I commanded.

His attention landed on Blake. "I have to hear him say it first."

Huffing, Blake held out his hand. "Go, MacCabe, before I change my mind." Connor shook his hand and I hugged him one more time before he took off at a sprint.

"Hey," Blake hollered after him. Connor stopped and turned around. "If you bring any kind of trouble to our doorstep, I will hunt you down and kill you. Got that?"

A wide grin spread across his face. "I'm not stupid enough to do that." He turned and disappeared just in time for the police to barge in through the gate.

"I'm ready to go home," I said.

Pulling me into his side, he kissed the side of my head. "Don't worry, you'll be back to California in no time."

I looked up at him and smiled. "Nah. I think it's time I found a place where I belonged."

CHAPTER 36

HADLEY

"So I'm good to go?" I asked the doctor.

She smiled over the file in her hands. "You are, as soon as you sign these for my two little girls. I'm pretty sure I'll never see you again after today," she said, handing me two pieces of hospital stationary. "It's not every day you meet someone who rose from the dead."

I signed the papers and handed them back to her. "I'm glad to be back. But what about him?" I asked, nodding over at Blake. He rolled his eyes and mumbled something under his breath about being fine. I had to laugh at the sight. He looked like Grumpy Cat in a hospital gown.

Dr. Reese chuckled. "We're just waiting on more of

his test results and then he'll be ready to go. It doesn't look like anything's broken."

"Because there's not," he grumbled. "I'm perfectly fine." They put us in the same room because he refused to let me out of his sight.

"Still, Mr. Evans, we have to make sure you're okay. You'll be out of here within the hour."

"What about my father? Is he awake yet?"

She closed my folder and held it to her chest. "He's in and out. We're flushing the drugs out of his system as we speak. They gave him a large dose. He's lucky to be alive."

I held back my tears. "Thanks, Dr. Reese. And Nick?"

"Doing surprisingly well. There was a clean exit wound. He'll be back on the ice before next season. He should be fine to leave tomorrow."

"Thank goodness," I replied, sighing with relief. He was probably tired of getting shot because of me.

"We contacted his sister so she should be here soon. She's your agent, right?"

And she had no clue I was alive. The media hadn't gotten hold of that story yet. "Yep, and it should be quite interesting when she sees me."

"I bet," she laughed, glancing down at her watch. "All right, let me check up on those test results and I'll be back."

Once she left, I climbed up on the bed with Blake. "I

never thought about how weird it's going to be to see everyone when we get back. It wouldn't surprise me if the paparazzi comes up with some stupid story about how I faked my own death to get media attention."

Blake snorted. "They can fuck themselves. We know the truth and that's all that matters." Wrapping his arm around my waist, he pulled me down next to him and held me.

"What am I going to say to my dad? I'm so confused right now."

He squeezed me. "You have to tell him how you feel. If he wasn't in a hospital bed right now, I'd have beaten the shit out of him for what he did. However, it's up to you to forgive him."

"What if I can't?" Tears fell down my cheeks onto the pillow. What my father did would forever impact my life. Nothing in the world could take away those scars.

"You will one day. He just needs to know he doesn't have to protect you anymore. You have me for that."

"Does that mean you're going to be my bodyguard?" I quipped.

He pressed his groin into my back. "I'll do more than protect your body, princess."

I slapped his arm playfully and shook my head. "What about your undercover work? You won't be able to do as much." I turned in his arms and faced him. His fingers grazed along my cheek and then he leaned over and kissed me.

"I don't care about any of it. I want to be with you and I'll do that any way I can. I can't trust anyone else to protect you."

"It's because nobody can. *You're* the only one I trust with my life. I don't want anyone else."

He smirked. "You sure you won't be embarrassed to be seen with me?"

"Never," I murmured truthfully.

"Even if I wear Mexican pointy boots on the red carpet?" His lips spread wide and I laughed.

"Who knows, you might start a trend. But then again, it might draw too much attention. I'll be fighting women off left and right." We both laughed at the thought.

His face turned serious. "I need you to do me a favor."

I nodded. "Anything, just name it."

"Be patient. I don't know what it's like to be with someone like you, to be followed around and hounded constantly. And you know my ranch isn't the fanciest of places, but it's home for me. It's just not what you're used to."

I placed a finger to his lips. "I don't need fancy or lavish, Blake. All I want is my dirty ol' cowboy, some hay for us to roll around in, and a horse to ride off into the sunset. I'll even clean out the stalls and go hiking every day if you want me to. That's where I belong . . . with you."

Pulling my hand away, he covered me with his body and kissed me. "I love you, Hadley. So much it fucking hurts."

"I know the feeling."

"Are you ready for this?" I asked.

Blake groaned. "Not really, but it's now or never. I'll just cover my ears when she screams."

"She already is . . . I can hear her all the way from here." She was probably yelling at Nick because he wouldn't tell her what happened. I wanted him to wait until Blake and I were in there with him.

Thankfully, all of Blake's tests came back normal. We had both been discharged from the hospital, but we stayed around so I could keep an eye on my dad and also wait for Felicity. We weren't going to be able to stay long because the more people who saw me at the hospital, the more rumors were going to start circulating.

"All right, here we go." When I opened the door, she was still yelling. Nick smiled the entire time and his grin got bigger when he saw us walk in.

"What the hell are you smiling about?" Felicity

snapped. "There's nothing funny about getting shot . . . *again*."

"Maybe if he knew what the fuck he was doing, it wouldn't have happened in the first place," Blake joked.

I smacked him on the arm and he laughed. Felicity huffed and glanced quickly over her shoulder and then did a double take, mouth gaping wide.

"Surprise," I announced nervously.

She stared at me in horror and then backed up to the wall with her hand over her heart.

Her body was shaking all over. "How? How is this possible?"

"It's a long story, and thankfully, Nick and Blake were there to help me." Nick held out his hand and he pulled me over. "You doing okay?" I asked him.

"Great. Ready to play some hockey." He rolled his shoulder and winced. "Or maybe I'll give it a few days." He laughed.

Felicity sidled over, reaching out her hand until she touched me. Eyes wide, she squeezed my arm. "Is it really you?" Tears streamed down her cheeks. When I nodded, she flung her arms around my neck. "Don't you ever do this to me again!"

We fell over onto Nick's bed and I laughed. "Believe me, I don't plan on it."

"Wait," she growled, pulling away from me and glaring at Nick. "Did you know she was alive this whole time?"

His smile faded. "No. Evans and I didn't find out until we were in Burnsville. Then we had to plan a rescue mission. I'm talking guns, mafia, you name it. They could make a movie out of this shit. Actually, they probably will."

"Are you serious? Did anyone get killed?"

Nick and I both stared at each other and I knew he felt the same betrayal I did. Blake was the one who answered. "A few people did, including Tristan. He's the one who was behind everything from the very beginning. He killed Scott and shot Nick, all in hopes of getting Connor put in as her bodyguard. That way he could have access to her."

"Fucking *Tristan*? Tristan Doherty? What the fuck? What about that Dane guy?" she asked, focusing on me.

"He was a regular ol' stalker and ended up being at the right place at the wrong time. He was innocent, except for trespassing on my property. Tristan admitted to being the one who broke in that night though."

She fell down in the chair, her mouth open in shock. "I can't believe this. This is some serious stuff right here. Do you realize how many people are going to want to talk to you when we get back? I'm talking the news, talk shows, et cetera. You'll be booked up for months."

I glanced up at Blake and he put his arm around me. "What do you think?" I asked him. She was right, there were going to be a lot of people who wanted to talk to me.

Blake squeezed my shoulder and sighed. "It's up to you, princess. I'll do whatever you need me to do."

Felicity's brows furrowed. "Something you need to tell me?" she asked.

Smiling wide, I wrapped my arm around Blake's waist. "I'll stay in town until everything calms down. Then afterward, I'm going home . . . to Wyoming."

She gasped. "You're leaving us?"

Nick nodded in understanding which gave me the courage I needed. I was so afraid of losing him as a friend, but after everything that happened, I felt like we were closer than ever. He might have even won Blake over in the process. I could dream, anyway.

"I am, but I'm still going to sing. So schedule up my concerts and do your thing. I'll be there," I promised.

"What about your producer? Recording your music?"

"I guess I'll have to cross that bridge when I get to it."

CHAPTER 37

HADLEY

Nick and Felicity left to go back to California and ever since being back, they'd been the main headline on every single news station on TV. My time was going to come. There were people parked outside of the hospital to see us, but I hadn't left the building. For two days, Blake and I stayed hidden in the hospital, waiting for my dad to fully wake up. I couldn't leave without him.

We had tried to eat lunch in the cafeteria but there were reporters everywhere pretending to eat lunch. Luckily, Dr. Reese took pity on me and let us hide out in an empty room, just down the hall from my father.

"Is Tyla okay with taking care of everything while

you're gone?" I asked.

Blake finished taking a sip of his soda and nodded. "She has Jerrod to help her in the mornings. Nightshade will be glad to see us come back though."

"What about the new horse you're supposed to be training? Tyla doesn't mind putting in the extra work?"

He snorted. "She's getting paid for it. Trust me, she'll be fine. I have ten million in my bank account to help with that."

"You deserve a whole hell of a lot more, after doing what you did. My dad will be indebted to you, as am I."

He winked. "There's plenty of ways for you to pay me back. As soon as we get home, I'll start collecting."

I leaned forward and rubbed my hand up his thigh. "Do we have to wait until we get home?"

"Don't start something you can't finish, princess." He growled and grasped my hand, pushing it over the bulge growing rapidly under his jeans.

I pulled my hand back and frowned. "You're right, it would be *risky* here." I stood up and walked over to the door. "I mean, anyone could walk in at any time." Pulling my sundress up and resting it on top of my ass, I turned to give him the view. Spreading my legs apart, I placed my hands on the door. "If only there was a way we could do it quickly . . ."

Looking over my shoulder, I saw his darkened eyes staring at my ass, mouth slackened in disbelief. I wiggled it a little and said, "Whatcha waitin' for, cowboy?"

"Fuck, baby. Are you serious right now?" He stood and stalked toward me, unzipping his jeans and freeing his cock. Pumping it a few times, he came up behind me and grabbed my ass cheeks. Rubbing his length between them, he groaned. "I can't believe this is happening. You're so fucking hot."

Leaning back into him, I turned my head and kissed him hard. He continued to move against me and the heat between us was consuming me alive. I leaned into the wall and pushed into him.

Pulling my panties to the side, he aligned himself and thrust home. It felt like he was splitting me in half and I almost fell to my knees with pleasure. Pushing into me hard and fast, he ground his fingers into my hips to hold me tight.

I bit my lip to keep my moans from getting too loud, but our bodies banging against the door and Blake's grunts were too loud for anyone walking by not to notice.

"Jesus," he bit out. "I'm gonna come."

I pushed back into him, over and over, until he wrapped his arms around me and bit my shoulder, his whole body jerking with release. Hearing him come undone sent me spiraling into my own orgasm. He continued to move, as I spasmed and bucked along his length. I stood straight and he held me up, chuckling and nipping at my ear.

I joined in his exhilaration, giggling at my actions. "Well, *that* happened."

"That it did, you little vixen. I never knew you had it in you." He pulled out of me and turned me around.

I broke into laughter when I saw him standing there in a T-shirt, with his pants and boxers around his ankles, in a hospital room that wasn't even ours.

A knock sounded on the door and my eyes went wide. The door started to open and I pushed Blake into the bathroom and shut the door. Dr. Reese poked her head inside and I spun around to face her.

"Hadley, your father's awake. He's asking for you."

"Oh! That's wonderful news." I glanced down to make sure my dress was covering everything. "Blake, honey, did you hear that?" I called to him in the bathroom.

He came out of the bathroom all zipped up and I breathed a sigh of relief. "I did. Is he fully alert?"

"Yes, he's wide awake," the doctor said, holding the door open for us. Heart racing, we followed her down the hall toward my father's room. "We have crutches for him so he can get up and walk around. The leg wound is healing nicely."

We stopped outside of his door. I wasn't ready to go in just yet. "Are there any complications from the drugs I should know about?"

She shook her head. "Nothing I could find. I think he's just sick with worry over you."

"Thanks, Dr. Reese. When do you think I can take him home?"

"Tomorrow," she replied with a smile. "I gotta run, but I'll check on you guys later this afternoon."

Taking a deep breath, I propped against the door and watched her disappear down the hall.

"Do you want me to go in there with you?" Blake asked.

"Yes. He owes us both an apology." I found the courage to press the handle down and open the door. My father watched us walk in with tears in his eyes and it broke my heart.

Blake nudged me forward. "Go to him," he whispered, standing back as I closed the distance, taking a seat beside my father's bed.

His skin was pale and he looked older than his usual self. The last time I saw him so vulnerable was after my mother died. After that, he'd turned into a powerhouse who had to control everything around him.

"I'm so sorry, Hadley." He broke down in sobs. "I never wanted to hurt you. All I wanted was to keep my baby girl safe."

"And look where that got us," I countered.

He nodded. "I know. I put everyone's lives in danger, mostly yours. The one person I wanted to protect ended up being the one I almost destroyed."

"If it wasn't for Blake, I'd be dead. He's the one who found me."

His gaze landed on Blake. "How did you find her?"

Blake's jaw tensed. "I have my ways, Mr. Rivers. I wasn't going to rest until I found out what happened to her."

My father held out his hand. "I owe you an apology, young man. I don't think I'll ever be able to repay you after what you did."

Blake stared at his hand, then shook it. "I accept your apology, but I don't accept the fact you tried to take Hadley away from everyone, from me. It was selfish."

"Blake," I hissed.

Holding his hands up, he backed away. "I'm done. That's all I wanted to say."

"No, he's right," my father agreed. "I know you won't forgive me now, but I hope in time you'll understand my reasoning. You're all I have left in this world. When Tristan told me he was responsible for all the threats, I felt like a fool. I played right into his hands."

I gasped. "What all did he tell you?"

He reached for my hand and I let him take it. "Everything. He said he was going to have me killed as soon as you left for Ireland. When I arrived at the house, I could feel that something wasn't right, especially when they wouldn't let me see you. I tried to find you and that's when everything went blurry."

"They drugged you just like they drugged me. Connor was the one who told me everything," I revealed.

"Where is he?" he asked.

I glanced back at Blake and he nodded. "Connor's dead, Dad. Just like everyone else who was involved."

"He never hurt you did he?"

"No," I gasped. "Connor was actually one of the good guys. He might have been on the bad side, but he protected me."

"So what happens now?" he murmured, squeezing my hand. "Do you think you can forgive me?"

Tears fell down my cheeks. I was still angry at him for what he did, but he was my father. I loved him more than anything. "On one condition." He lifted his brows in response. "I want you to let me live my life. No more finding me bodyguards, or trying to make decisions for me. All of that is done. If someone calls threatening my life, you tell them to eat a dick." Blake snorted and my father chuckled. "What I'm saying is, I'm going to live my life the way I want to live it. No more interference. Can you do that?"

Closing his eyes, he nodded. "I promise."

"There's one other thing," Blake interrupted. My father and I both focused our attention on him. "Our stories need to be straight. If word gets out about your involvement with the mafia, you could face jail time. For the sake of Hadley, and your reputation, you need to say you had no part in it."

My father blew out a nervous breath. "I can do that. Do you think I can get away with it?"

Blake's gaze narrowed. "Maybe, as long as you keep your word to Hadley. Pull any of this shit again and I'll make sure it comes back to bite you on the ass."

"Is he always this brash?" my father asked me.

Giggling, I looked up at Blake and smiled. "Always, but that's one of the reasons I love him."

CHAPTER 38

HADLEY

(Two Weeks Later)

"Hi everyone, and welcome to The Helen Carpenter Show," Helen announced to the audience. Helen Carpenter was not only a TV host, but an actress as well. She was in her early forties with short blonde hair, bright blue eyes, and had a love for designer pant suits. Her show was the most popular one on TV and Felicity thought it'd be the perfect place to make a comeback. Helen took the seat beside me, her eyes wide and full of excitement. "I have to say Miss Rivers, I'm honored you agreed to be on the show after everything that's happened. It's your first appearance since then, isn't it?"

"Yes," I agreed. "But I love your show. When you asked me, I couldn't possibly turn down the chance."

She winked at me and smiled. "Well, I appreciate that, and I'm sure our audience does as well. I know we don't want to spend the whole show talking about what happened, but I have to know, was it scary?"

"Oh my goodness, yes," I explained. "Everyone thought I was dead. Who in the world is going to go searching for someone who's supposed to be dead?"

"Obviously someone did. I heard you met him when you were in protective custody. Why don't you tell me about that?"

I burst out laughing. "Yes, that was interesting. Let me tell you, I hated him when we first met. He was nothing but a dirty cowboy who liked to give me a hard time." Blake shook his head and grinned when I glanced at him behind the stage.

"What all did he do?" Helen asked. From the get go, I knew they wanted to know about my relationship with Blake. He was still a mystery to them.

"For starters, he made me clean the horse stalls in his barn," I told the crowd.

They all laughed, oohing and aahing as I continued to discuss Blake, and my entire stay on his ranch. Their favorite part was when I'd brought up the boots.

"That's right folks," Helen exclaimed excitedly. "While I was backstage with Hadley, she showed me some pictures she took. Apparently, her new beau is trying to start a new trend. Why don't we take a look at this?" She nodded at one of the TV producers and then a picture popped up on the screen. It was of Blake in his Mexican pointy boots. The crowd burst into laughter and a ton of them whistled. Blake's mouth dropped when he saw it.

"Ladies, look at that handsome stud. Much different than the clean cut Blake we've seen the past couple of weeks," Helen said. Another picture popped up of him in a suit, from when we were walking into a restaurant for dinner.

Blake chuckled when more of the ladies started whistling at his picture. "I have to say, I miss his cowboy hat and jeans."

"What is with those boots though?" The picture bounced back to the one with him in the boots.

"He lost a bet. I picked them out myself."

"Very nice," she laughed. "So what are your plans now that you're alive?"

Taking a deep breath, I smiled at the crowd. "I plan on singing again, but I'll also be making some changes in my life. And one of those changes, will happen right here on this show today." My heart started to race; especially when I looked over at Blake. He had no clue what was going on.

Felicity disappeared and then walked out onto the

stage, carrying the guitar Blake gave me. His eyes went wide when he realized what was going on. "Knock 'em dead," she whispered, passing me the guitar.

I pulled the strap over my shoulder. "Thanks."

Helen sat back in her chair. "So are you ready to tell the audience what the surprise is?" she asked.

The crowd had given me their undivided attention, including Blake. I was nervous as hell, but I was ready. If there was anything I learned over the past couple of months, it was to get over my fears. Today was the perfect day to start.

I took a deep breath and turned my body toward the crowd. "For years, I've performed in front of thousands of people, in different cities across the country, but never have I gotten on stage and sang something new. The song I will sing today is something I wrote a couple of months ago. It's about a very special person in my life. If it wasn't for him, I wouldn't be here today."

Strumming my fingers down the strings, I glanced over his way. "It's called *My Gray-Eyed Cowboy*." Felicity jumped up and down and grabbed his arm, but he didn't even notice her pulling on him. Drawing in a deep breath, I blew it out slowly and began. Music always came so easy to me, it was part of my soul. I wanted to look out at the crowd, but I couldn't take my eyes away from Blake.

He loves me, he loves me not.
Oh, how I wish I knew.
We haven't known each other long,
But when I'm with him,
I feel like I belong.
He loves me, he loves me not.
My gray-eyed cowboy, I want to know. (Please tell me)

Your heart may never be tamed,
But I am not afraid.
Will you love me if I leave, will you love me if I stay.
Dear gray-eyed cowboy, please show me the way.

Time has passed, a new life upon us.
So many things to see, so many things to do.
I want to stay in your arms,
And never let go.
My gray-eyed cowboy, I want to know. (Please tell me)

Your heart may never be tamed,
But I am not afraid.
Will you love me if I leave, will you love me if I stay.
Dear gray-eyed cowboy, please show me the way.

You may love me now, but can you promise me forever.
If there's one thing I can say,
It would be this . . .

I promise to love you, I promise to stay.
Never again will I leave you.
My heart is yours, your heart is mine.
My gray-eyed cowboy, thank you for showing me the way.

The whole room was silent. A tear fell down my cheek and I wiped it away quickly before turning my gaze to the crowd. I didn't know what to do or what to say, so I sat there waiting, as if I was on trial. I guess I kind of was. No one had ever heard the song before and now my fate rested on what the audience thought of it.

They jumped to their feet in applause, screaming and hollering my name, and I released the breath I hadn't realized I was holding.

"Wow," Helen exclaimed, "That was amazing. I could feel your emotions in it. I know that's what we all love about your music. You put so much heart and soul into it."

"Thanks. I like to write music about the people I care about. It makes it special."

Helen smiled and gazed out at the crowd. "I know I'm not the only one who can't wait to hear more. Why don't we make things a little more interesting and bring out this gray-eyed cowboy? What do you say people?"

The audience went crazy, clapping their hands and whistling. Eyes wide, I turned to Blake, knowing he was going to hate coming out there. Instead, he winked at me as one of the producers hooked a microphone to his button down shirt. What was going on?

He walked out on stage and waved at everyone as he took the seat beside me. Leaning over, he kissed me and whispered over the loud applause, "Love the song. Thank you for singing it to me. You need to do it more often." He put his arm around me and I snuggled into his side.

"I will," I murmured, winking up at him.

Helen reached over and shook his hand. "Blake Evans, it's good to have you on the show. I know a lot of people in the world want to meet Hadley's hero, or better yet, her gray-eyed cowboy. Where's your boots?"

"Soon to be burning in a fire the second we get home," he joked. "I think I need to get Hadley a pair to wear at her next concert."

I snorted. "Don't think so."

The crowd laughed and Helen giggled. "That'd be pretty epic. But Blake, I know the world's been dying to ask you this question." She glanced out at the crowd and then back to him. "How did you even think to go searching for Hadley? What made you think she wasn't dead?"

His arm tensed around me as he went into detail about hearing of my death, and the struggle he endured thinking I was gone forever. Over the next five minutes, he answered questions about the mission to find me, how he was dealing with the paparazzi, and even more questions about his boots. The crowd adored him. But how could they not?

The show was about to be over and I couldn't wait to get off stage and head back home. Blake and I hadn't been back to Wyoming at all since the rescue.

"Ladies and gentlemen, we have a few minutes left and I do believe Blake has something he'd like to say." She looked at him and he acknowledged her with a nod.

This was a surprise to me.

The stage lights brightened, and the lights over the audience dimmed. Blake stood, then got down on one knee. Gasps erupted from the women in the audience.

I clasped a hand over my mouth. "What are you doing?"

Felicity came out, handing him a small black box, winking at me before scampering away.

Blake squeezed my hands, his gray eyes swirling with raw emotion. "The day you showed up on my doorstep, I took one look at you and knew you were going to be trouble." Snickers could be heard from the audience and I smiled.

"I didn't want to care about you, but you made it impossible. I fell in love with you, knowing you could never be happy with a guy like me, or at least I thought you couldn't. That's why I'm here today, in front of all these people and the world, to ask you two questions."

Lifting my hand, he kissed it gently, his gray gaze never swaying from mine. "First, do you think you could be happy with a guy like me?"

Lips trembling, I nodded vigorously. "Yes," I whispered.

"That leaves just one more question." Taking a deep breath, he blew it out and opened the box.

"Oh my God," I cried. Warm tears fell down my cheeks. It wasn't just any diamond ring in that box . . . it was my mother's.

He pulled it out and held it up in the air. "I promise from today on to protect you, body and soul. I won't be happy until I know you're mine for the rest of my life. So, with that . . . Hadley Rivers, would you do me the honor of being my wife?"

"Yes," I burst out. "Yes, oh my God, yes."

Beaming, his eyes lit up as he placed the ring on my finger and lifted me in his arms. The crowd exploded into cheers and applause. "That was fast. You sure you don't need to think about it?" he teased.

I shook my head. "You're all I want, Blake Evans. There's no thinking twice. The real question is, will you be happy with me, with my life?"

He kissed me again. "As long as I have you, I'll let nothing come between us."

"Promise?"

"On my life."

CHAPTER 39

HADLEY
(Eight Months Later)

Belonging to a small community was better than I thought it would be. When everyone around Jackson Hole first realized who I was, it was a little crazy, but now they treated me just like everyone else. I didn't have to worry about walking down the street and having a gazillion people trying to chase me down for autographs. However, a lot of that was probably due to Blake always being with me.

"Do I *have* to be blindfolded?" I asked. For months, Blake had had contractors and builders out at our house, designing and constructing a separate house of sorts. It was almost like a small version of his ranch, just enough room for maybe two bedrooms. I had no clue what was going in there or what it was for. Today was reveal day. "You're not going to invite my dad to live here are you?"

Chuckling, Blake guided me through the door. "Fuck that shit. I might be impressed with how he's butted out of your life, but I don't want the man living here. This is our space."

I breathed a sigh of relief. "Thank God. I love him to death, but I don't want him living here either." It took a few months for our relationship to get back on track, but I was glad to have him back in my life. He was trying hard to make up for what he did.

"Are you ready to see your surprise?"

"Yes," I squealed, jumping up and down. Blake took off the blindfold and I gasped. I stood in the living room and gazed around. "It's so beautiful, Blake." There was a kitchen off to the right and a set of stairs to the left. "But, what is it for?"

Taking my hand, he walked me through the house. "Now that you're here with me full-time, I know you still have work to do and people you want to see. If your dad, Felicity, or anyone else wants to visit, they can stay out here, away from us. But that's not the real reason either." There was a closed door down the hall and he stopped in front of it. "This room is for you." He opened the door and I froze in awe.

"Holy shit." It was a recording studio, filled with top of the line equipment.

"Now you won't have to fly to California to record. We can have your producers come out here."

I fiddled with the dials on the control surface and sat down. "This is amazing. How did you think to do this?"

He sat down beside me. "I figured it'd help cut down on your travel time. Plus, you can always come in here and sing in privacy. I know you like to have your space when you're writing."

Grasping his face in my hands, I kissed him. "You know I don't have that fear anymore. I love singing to you and talking to you about my songs."

"And I love listening to you. But I want you to know you have this space, if you need it," he murmured.

"Thank you. You have no idea how much this means to me." I took one last look around and smiled. "Let me guess, you used a decent-sized chunk of that ten million on this?"

Smirking, he lifted me up into his arms. "I figured I'd spend it on you. It's a good investment, is it not?"

"Yes, definitely. The more time I get to spend at home the better."

Our wedding, only one week away, was going to be at our house, but the ceremony would be outside. It was more of a secret affair and only a dozen or so people were invited, including Felicity and Nick. I couldn't wait to see them again. Nick was in a serious relationship already, and planned on popping the question while in

Wyoming.

Grabbing my hand, Blake pulled me outside and across the yard. When we got to the barn, he winked. "I have another surprise for you. You're going to love this."

"Oh yeah? How *much* am I going to love it?" He chuckled and I had a feeling I knew what he was up to. "Does it involve ropes? Maybe a little sexy time in the hay? It's definitely been too long since we got dirty in the barn."

"Ugh, I didn't need to hear that," a voice griped from behind.

Blake burst out laughing and I yelped, slapping a hand to my chest. The voice didn't belong to just anyone; it came from a certain Irish mobster. Only now, he wasn't in his usual attire, but in a pair of jeans, a T-shirt, and a cowboy hat.

I closed my eyes and then opened them up again, convinced I was going crazy. "Okay, I'm not hallucinating. What the hell are you doing here?" Over the past few months, he'd sent emails to check up on me, but I had no clue where he was.

Connor rolled his eyes. "What? You've never seen an Irish cowboy?"

"Not exactly." Blake tried to hold back a laugh and failed. "Why didn't you tell me he was coming?" I asked.

"I wanted it to be a surprise. Plus, I needed a new

ranch hand. Tyla will love bossing him around." He and Connor shared a look I couldn't decipher; there was something he wasn't telling me.

"Are you sure that's it?"

Sighing, he pulled me into his arms. "It's nothing for you to worry about. I have a lot of enemies out there and having the extra security will give me peace of mind."

"Do you think the Irish will try to retaliate?"

He shook his head. "I don't think they will, but if they do, Connor will know how to spot them. It might not be so bad having the old man around."

Connor snorted. "Old man, my ass. I've only got you by five years, you shithead."

They bantered back and forth and I couldn't help but laugh. Having Connor there was going to be interesting, but I knew I'd enjoy it.

Staring up at Blake, I couldn't help but feel completely and utterly at peace. The thought of living with him for the rest of my life filled me with joy. He was mine and I was his. He had me completely roped in.

THE END

HIGH-SIDED (Armed & Dangerous)
Logan's story
Coming August 2016

ABOUT THE AUTHOR

NEW YORK TIMES and USA Today Bestselling author, L.P. Dover, is a southern belle residing in North Carolina along with her husband and two beautiful girls. Before she even began her literary journey she worked in Periodontics enjoying the wonderment of dental surgeries.

Not only does she love to write, but she loves to play tennis, go on mountain hikes, white water rafting, and you can't forget the passion for singing. Her two number one fans expect a concert each and every night before bedtime and those songs usually consist of Christmas carols.

Aside from being a wife and mother, L.P. Dover has written countless novels including her Forever Fae series, the Second Chances series, and her standalone novel, Love, Lies, and Deception. Her favorite genre to read is romantic suspense and she also loves writing it. However, if she had to choose a setting to live in it would have to be with her faeries in the Land of the Fae.

L.P. Dover is represented by Marisa Corvisiero of Corvisiero Literary Agency.

Also, keep reading to get a sneak peek at
The Reeducation of Savannah McGuire
by Heidi McLaughlin

THE REEDUCATION
OF
SAVANNAH MCGUIRE

By: Heidi McLaughlin

© 2015

Chapter 1 – Tyler

Savannah McGuire, the girl who was taken from Rivers Crossing years ago by her power-hungry mother, is due to return. I'm excited and nervous, a deadly combination. Diagnosis: pure anxiety. My palms are sweaty, my leg is bouncing up and down and I don't know why. Sure, it's been five years since we've seen or spoken to each other, but her coming back here shouldn't make me feel like I'm about to go on a date with Miss America.

When I see the old Greyhound bus come rumbling down the road, I straighten in my seat, clutching the steering wheel until my knuckles are white with tension. I've known about her return for a week now, but haven't let the news set in that my one-time best friend is returning. Half of me thought this day would never happen because something would prevent her from coming home. I'm still not convinced that it will be her getting off the bus in a few seconds.

The Greyhound comes to a halt, its brakes squealing from the pressure. The door swings open and my eyes instantly scan the windows to see if I can spot Savannah. I hold my breath when I see candy-apple-red heels hitting the last step before reaching the cracked pavement. Her long blonde hair sways lightly from the exhaust blowing behind her. It's stifling out and this is as much of a breeze as she's going to get. She moves her head back and forth just like those stupid hair commercials my mom is always watching. She looks up and down the road before setting her hands on her hips. I shake my head, knowing that this ain't my Savannah.

The bus isn't pulling away so I know Savannah is still on it. I lean into the steering wheel to get a better look. The blonde side steps and allows the next passenger off the bus. *This* is my Savannah, with her shoulder-length brown hair and oversized clothes. She was always wearing her Uncle Bobby's shirts when we were younger, afraid of how her body was changing. Jeremiah used to call her Mouse, and he'll be happy to see that she hasn't changed.

After throwing my shoulder into the door, I hop out and clap my hands once out of excitement. I rush over to Savannah and pick her up, twirling her around. "God, I've missed you. Are you ready to have the best summer of your life?"

"Uh, put me down, please."

Fulfilling her request, but not ready to let go, I pull her into a hug. Her hands push firmly against my chest as she steps away. Savannah brushes off her clothes as if I've contaminated them. The blonde clears her throat and smiles. I roll my eyes. I know it's probably real hard for her to stand here and watch this reunion, but it's not my fault that her family isn't here on time. By her looks, I'm sure she gets all the attention she wants.

"Are you ready to go, Savannah?"

"Yes, I am." The blonde speaks up. I look at her. With her hand on her hip, she taps her toe on the ground and smirks.

"Look ma'am, I'm sorry your kinfolk aren't here to get ya and if ya want we can wait, but I'm sure they'll be along soon." I reach for Savannah's bags, but her hand stops me.

"I don't know you," she says quietly as she removes my hand from her suitcase.

"Excuse me?" I question, as I stand tall. "What do you mean you don't know me?"

She shrugs. "I don't know you and my name's not Savannah."

"Mine is though, and just wait until I tell my Uncle Bobby how you tried to take someone else home, Tyler King."

Slowly turning and eyeing the statuesque blonde, my heart stops beating. The smirk is back, or it never left. I step closer so I can see what happened to the mousy brunette I used to know. Her gaze follows mine and I look her over. She's taller, leaner and, besides the obvious hair color change, looks nothing like she did when she left here. Her teeth are straight and missing the metal that used to clog her mouth. There's no way this woman is only seventeen years old.

I swallow hard and break eye contact. This ain't gonna be good. When I thought she was this other girl, I pictured us hanging out. Now that I'm looking at her, the hanging out idea doesn't seem to be the best thing for me. One thing's for sure: New York did a number on my Savannah.

"Wow, Savannah."

She nods, pursing her lips. "It's Vanna," she informs me as she stalks past me toward my truck. I follow her and mentally scold myself when my eyes fall on her cotton-covered ass. The mousy-non-Savannah mocks me in disgust. I run my hand over the back of my neck and sigh.

"Sorry 'bout that," I say. "Um… do you need a ride?"

She shakes her head and I deduce that I'm better off just leaving her. I've already embarrassed her and myself enough to last us a lifetime. I pick up Savannah's bags and hustle back to the truck. I have a feeling it's gonna be one long summer and once her Uncle Bobby sees her he's gonna flip. She's going to be every man's wet dream in a forty-mile radius and I just know I'm going to be tasked with taking care of her. Just call me the glorified babysitter of the mousy farm girl turned New York socialite.

I remember the day she left. I thought her momma was joking when she said they were moving, so when they packed their bags and got into the car, I was left standing there, stunned. I was so hurt that I refused to say good-bye. We didn't promise to write or even call each other. We were too young for those types of commitments. Watching her being driven away from me is my most vivid memory and one that has been replaying in my mind for the past week.

I was fifteen when she left. We'd grown up together, attending the same school, church and having Sunday suppers on her uncle's wrap-around porch. Our mommas always joked that we'd end up married to each other as soon as she turned eighteen and we'd start spitting out babies. After a while, I just believed them. It seemed like destiny. That was until my teenage hormones kicked in, and when I discovered girls, Savannah wanted nothing to do with me. She caught me a time or two with my hands in places they shouldn't have been and each time she'd just pretend like nothing was happening.

Even though our mommas wanted us to get married, there is an age difference between us and I matured faster. Savannah was quiet and shy, never really showing any interest in anything but her horse. Living in a small town, people have expectations and there was one on her and me, but it wasn't like I could take her out on a date or anything. Looking at her now, I wish I could've.

I climb into the cab of my truck and pull the door shut. She jumps in and clutches her purse tightly to her body. I let my hand dangle over the steering wheel thinking about all the things I want to say to her. Right now the only thing forming is the idiotic sentence of "damn, you grew up", but I have a feeling that will earn me a slap and I'd rather save that for later in the barn. I instantly chide myself for thinking I'll get her to the barn like that. She just got here and I'm sure she has a rich pretty boy waiting on her back home.

"Hello, Savannah. Long time no see." She adjusts slightly, turning farther away from me, and stares out her window. Her mood has changed from somewhat friendly to icy cold. I don't blame her. The warm reception I gave the other woman was probably what she was expecting and didn't get.

"It's Vanna."

I want to laugh at how straight-laced she sounds but hold back. Something tells me she's turned into a spitfire and that would be the spark to set her off. I've already pissed her off enough for one day. Her uncle said something about her getting into trouble one too many times at school and that her momma is too busy with her job to keep her under control. Apparently the answer was to send her back to where she got her start, even if she's not going to fit in around these parts anymore.

"Savannah," I reply purposely. There's no way in hell I'm calling her *Vanna* after that middle-aged letter turner that my grandma watches nightly.

She huffs, but doesn't say anything. I get the impression that she's used to getting her way, especially with men. Sadly for her, life doesn't work like that in these parts.

"How far 'til my uncle's house?"

I look out the windshield, pretending I need to gauge the distance. I shrug. "Twenty minutes or so."

"Well, shouldn't we get moving?"

I shake my head and mentally kick my own ass for how this day has started. I'd like a redo, please. Hell yeah I'd jump out of this truck and scoop her up in my arms if I knew what she had grown into, but I was remembering my reserved Savannah, not the model sitting next to me.

Cranking my key to start the engine, I'm happy for the loud roar to drown out my thoughts about her and us… in the barn. It's never gonna happen so I just need to stop thinking about it. I need to remember mud pie, cow tippin' and catching lightnin' bugs.

"Hang on tight, sweetheart." I press down on the gas as I throw my truck into drive. She slams back against the seat, her door barely closed. I'm trying not to laugh but her high-pitched squeal is cracking me up. She's turned into such a girly girl that someone is going to have to break her out of it and it ain't gonna be me.

Made in the USA
Lexington, KY
28 October 2015